"Sera."

"Alex."

They both laughed.

Alex grabbed her by the arms and pulled her into an alcove as passengers jostled their way in and out of the city's bus station. "I had a great time this weekend."

The heat moved up Sera's neck and onto her cheeks at the memories. Alex pulled her closer, although the crowds seemed to have thinned. "As far as I'm concerned, this weekend was Cy's loss and my gain."

Her body seemed to move toward Alex's as if she were on a magic carpet. "I think so, too."

"You asked if I thought you could return to school at your age. Personally, I think anyone can return to school at any age. If the school offers you a scholarship again, I think you'd be crazy not to accept." His lips were now just inches from hers. And then he kissed her. A proper goodbye kiss. Not a spur-of-the-moment, wish-he-would-stop-talking kiss.

Dear Reader,

I'm happy to share with you *Deal of a Lifetime*, book number three in the Bear Meadows series. Thank you for sticking with me as together we see where life takes these characters. As always, a special thank-you to the team at Harlequin and your invaluable suggestions for keeping the story on track. Kudos for creating a beautiful book presentation for the Heartwarming line.

I hope you're enjoying reading about the characters and their journeys as much as I enjoy writing about them. Just like the people we interact with daily, book characters behave a certain way and have unique personalities. We can only begin to understand them once we understand their deepest fears and greatest hopes.

In *Deal of a Lifetime*, Serafina Callahan feels an obligation to stay on the family farm. If life had played out differently, Sera's dreams and aspirations would have taken her far away.

Last Chance Farm is only a few years away from receiving Century Farm designation. But today's family farm looks nothing like the family farm of my grandparents' generation. Sustaining a family is hardly possible without someone having an outside income or, in the case of Last Chance Farm, reinventing the concept.

The question for Sera is...where does obligation to family end and the fulfillment of one's dreams begin, especially given her feelings for the hero, Alex?

T.R.

HEARTWARMING

Deal of a Lifetime

T. R. McClure

ISBN-13: 978-0-373-36852-5

Deal of a Lifetime

This edition published by arrangement with Harlequin Books S.A.

For questions and comments about the quality of this book, please contact us at CustomerService@Harlequin.com.

Printed in U.S.A.

T. R. McClure wrote her first story when she was ten years old. A degree in psychology led to a career in human resources. Only after retirement did she pick up her pen and return to fiction. T.R. lives in central Pennsylvania with her husband of thirty-seven years. They share their country home with one horse, one cat, four beagles and Sunny the yellow Lab. T.R. is always up for travel adventures with her grown twin daughters. For more information and updates on new releases, visit www.trmcclure.com or follow the author on Twitter, @trmcclureauthor.

Books by T. R. McClure

Harlequin Heartwarming

An Allegheny Homecoming
Wanted: The Perfect Mom

To my husband and daughters, who surprised me with an awesome book birthday party for my first book. You pulled off the surprise!

Blaine, Kristen and Launa, you're awesome and I'm blessed to have you in my life.

CHAPTER ONE

HER GREAT-GRANDMOTHER MUST have known what she was doing when she named their home Last Chance Farm, because the men in Serafina Callahan's family were all gamblers of one sort or another, her little brother included.

"What are you thinking?"

Sitting in one of a line of uncomfortable molded plastic chairs in the terminal lobby, Sera linked her hands over her belly and stared out the floor-to-ceiling window at the twin-engine turboprop, its propellers whirling to a stop. "I'm thinking no way would I climb on a soup can with wings in the middle of a hurricane and fly to Nashville."

Mirroring her stretched-out position, crossed ankles and all, Chance Callahan rested the toe of his boot against the battered guitar case, as if reassuring himself the instrument was still there, even though it was in plain sight of both of them. "We're going to Detroit first. It's not raining in Detroit."

"That makes no sense—" Sera slid her gaze up her brother's long legs to his mussed black hair "—but neither does April showers in May."

"Springtime in Pennsylvania. You never know what you're gonna get. No big deal." He shrugged.

She wasn't surprised. Her younger brother had his own theories about life. He did exactly as he pleased. But then the siblings had traveled different paths from the beginning. She would climb into the crook of an apple tree on a summer day to read, and he would swing from the branches, risking skinned knees and broken bones. "You know, I think you're the milkman's son. We can't be related."

Head leaning against the seat back, he turned in her direction. His eyes had that heavy-lidded look that made the girls scream when he was onstage. "We both have the Callahan hair. Thick, black and totally unmanageable. We're related."

Sera smoothed curly bangs back from her forehead and returned her gaze to the activities on the other side of the window. "Tell me about it."

Clad in a hooded poncho with *Ramp* written across the back in large black letters, a figure reached up to lower the staircase of the plane. April Madison appeared at the top of the stairs. She wore navy blue suit pants and a crisp white blouse. A red-white-and-blue-striped scarf looped around her neck. With a bright smile, she handed a clipboard to the agent on the ground.

"Did you know April Madison is working for Allegheny Commuter? She might be the last person you see before plummeting to the ground."

One corner of his mouth edged upward. "I can think of worse things."

"You hate April Madison."

"I hated her in high school. She dumped me for one of the Heaster twins. Now that Stan is serving three to ten, she's probably rethinking that decision."

Sera chuckled. "Ya think?" As always, she and her brother had reverted to familiar and comfortable conversation, like two neighbors who hadn't seen each other in a while. April backed away into the dark recesses of the cabin as passengers appeared in the open doorway. The first person off the plane was a young woman with frizzy red hair. Shoulders hunched against the rain, she clutched a portfolio in her left arm and gripped the railing with her hand.

"Dating any Southern belles?" Sera continued to watch the passengers, but her ear was attuned to any sound from the man next to her. He took a long time to answer.

"Not at the moment."

An alarm sounded at the back of her brain. Chance and women. Not a good combination when his career was supposed to be the focus. “Were you?”

“Let’s just say, at the present time, there is no special someone.” He shrugged and returned her gaze. The half smile was gone. “You?”

She raised her hands to the ceiling and directed an exasperated look in his direction. “There is such a multitude of men at the farm, I’m having trouble choosing.” The smile she was looking for returned when her little brother laughed. She had accomplished her mission.

“I keep telling you, you should get out more.” Chance scooted back in his seat, rested his arms on his thighs and stared at his guitar. “I saw the reassessment notice from the county on your desk.”

“Yep. Things just keep getting better and better.” Sera returned her gaze to the passengers exiting the plane just in time to see a tall man in a navy windbreaker stoop to emerge from the plane’s oval doorway. He stood at the top of the metal staircase, looking around as if surveying his domain. The wind ruffled his light brown hair. How nice to feel such confidence.

"Did the taxes go up?"

She tore her gaze from the confident man with the windblown hair. "Do cats have kittens?" Unlike the woman with the red hair, his wide shoulders were not at all hunched, as if the rain didn't exist. "Do taxes ever go down?"

The ticket agent announced boarding for Detroit. Chance stood, his lanky frame unraveling from the seat like the Slinky toy he used to play with on the front porch steps. Slapping his cowboy hat on his head, he slid her a look. "When I get my next gig—"

"Don't worry about it." Standing and facing her brother, she pressed a twenty-dollar bill into his hand. "Grab a snack in Detroit."

"Hey, I'm fine." He tried to give the money back.

"No, keep it. As Aunt Hope would say, you're skinny as a rail." Despite the joking, she did worry about her brother getting on the small plane in the middle of a rainstorm. Heck, she worried about small planes on sunny days. "Good luck with the audition."

They put their arms around each other; Sera patted his back twice before Chance pulled away. He shot her a look and then just as quickly glanced away. "Thanks, Sera. I feel like I should stick around, but this could be the one. It's the Blue Bird, you know?" His gaze rested on the guitar case at his feet.

Sera recognized the hopeful expression on her brother's handsome face. So what if he couldn't help her with expenses? He really did have a shot at the big time. Unlike her, he was willing to take the risk. She punched him in the shoulder. "Remember what Dad said."

"Love what you do." His smile lit his face, transforming him from the average twentysomething into a star. "Bye, sis." If looks were a prerequisite for becoming a country Western sensation, Chance

Callahan was well on his way. His deep, gravelly voice lent another level of sensuality to the man with the two-day growth of beard. He slung a carry-on over his shoulder, picked up the battered guitar case and joined the line of people headed for security.

Bypassing a long line, her brother slid his luggage on a conveyor belt and walked through the security gate without a qualm, shoes and all. Of course, he was prescreened. He had done the same thing many times over the last three years.

The passengers who had just left the recently arrived plane filed through a long, transparent walkway that emptied into the lobby. Sera picked up her poncho just as the young woman with the frizzy red hair emerged. With a shrill "Mommy," a little redheaded boy broke free from his father and ran into her arms. Hugs and kisses all around. Mom, Dad, toddler.

Watching the other passengers follow her brother onto the ramp, she wondered what adventures they were about to enjoy.

More than she, for sure. Sera turned away from the lucky passengers and headed for the bar. She dared not leave until the flight was in the air.

"YOU DON'T HAVE a reservation for Alexander Kimmel?" Alex stared at the young man with the unusual mop of unnaturally white-blond hair sticking up every which way. His name tag read Scooby, which somehow seemed appropriate. The car rental agent looked to be about ten years old.

Scooby flushed bright red. "I'm afraid not." He glanced at his computer. "However, I expect a car returned anytime now. Do you want to wait in the bar?" He flashed a toothy smile, displaying multicolored braces.

Alex wished for his sunglasses, packed away deep in his carry-on. The combination of the hair and the teeth was just too much. He gripped the edge of the counter with both hands. Surely he hadn't heard right. "Did you say you only have two cars?"

"Well, I'm just starting out." Throwing his shoulders back, he pointed to the sign behind him. Scooby's Rental Cars. "Before me, Shadow Falls Regional Airport didn't have a car rental."

Alex hated to point out the obvious to the enthusiastic car rental agent on the other side of the counter, but somebody had to give this guy a dose of reality. "But you don't have any cars to rent."

Scooby shrugged. "If I don't get my car back in time, there might be someone in the bar who can give you a ride."

Squeezing his eyes shut, Alex pinched the bridge of his nose, hoping to stave off the headache that threatened. He never should have come, never given in. Cyrus was supposed to pick him up. Instead, he had called, saying he had an emergency with a sick cow. A new vet was on call, and he had to be there. But the regional airport had a car rental agency. Alex could rent a car. With a deep breath,

Alex opened his eyes and looked around the lobby. So much for reality. "Where's the bar?"

Bar was spelled out in fake, multicolored glass in the top of a dark, wood-paneled door. Five backless stools, a short bar and three tiny red vinyl booths crowded a windowless space. Wheeling his suitcase next to the wall, Alex propped his hip on one stool at the end and glanced at the display of bottles behind the bar. One other customer hunched over a bottle at the far end of the bar. A curtain of curly black hair shielded her face.

"What can I get for you?" A middle-aged man in a faded green T-shirt and jeans wiped the counter in front of him.

Alex studied the labels, didn't see anything familiar, then tilted his head toward the lone customer. "I'll have what she's having."

Reaching into a glass-fronted cooler, the bartender plunked a sweaty brown bottle on the counter. "Headed in or out?"

He grabbed his rag and continued down the counter, wiping in a circular motion.

Alex took a long swig before answering, the tangy brew waking up his mouth. He set the bottle on the coaster. "In."

"Good thing." He snorted. "They just canceled the last flight in for the day." He tipped his chin to the ceiling. "Visibility. Where ya from?"

"New York."

He nodded, then pointed at the bottle in his hand. "I hear hard cider is getting popular in the city. True?"

Alex twisted the bottle around until he could read the label and then realized the hard cider was the same brand he had been drinking just the night before. "As a matter of fact, hard cider is becoming very popular."

"Do me a favor..." The bartender disappeared through a swinging door, reappearing a minute later with a plain brown bottle. "Try this and tell me what you think." He pulled three tumblers from under the counter. "Hey, Sera, want to try something?"

Sitting in the shadows, the woman looked up at the sound of her name. "Okay." She slid off the stool. "Just a little bit." She grabbed a yellow poncho and a big purse, and put everything on the stool next to Alex, then sat. She gave Alex a wary look before turning her gaze to the bartender.

"By the way, my name's Mike." The bartender smiled as he emptied the bottle into three glasses. He set one in front of Alex and one in front of the young woman. "This is a taste test."

Picking up the glass, she raised it to her lips.

"Hold on." Mike held up his glass and shared a big smile. "To success."

"To success." Alex clinked his glass with Mike's and then tipped his glass in the direction of the dark-haired woman. She looked at the glass, then at him and lightly touched her glass to his.

"To success."

Alex sipped the liquid, swirled it around in his mouth and nodded. "Not bad. You removed the label."

The bartender didn't answer, instead waiting for Sera to give her response. She held the glass under her nose and sniffed. "You made this, didn't you?"

He nodded. "I made this last fall. I call it Flying Apple. You like?"

"Very nice." She smiled.

Alex watched the exchange. The woman was obviously a regular. And she was capable of smiling. Just not in his direction.

"You're the first customers I've tried it on. My family drinks it, but they'll drink anything." Mike set a bowl of pretzels on the counter between Alex and the woman.

The door flew open. Scooby settled next to Sera. "I'll have what they're having, Mike."

"Nice try, buddy. You know you're not supposed to be sitting at the bar." Mike raised one eyebrow at the shaggy-haired entrepreneur.

Alex upended his glass. He had to give the young man credit. Not even old enough to drink and he was starting his own business.

"I'll just be a minute. I'm here on business." He leaned forward and addressed Alex. "I just got a call. The car I was supposed to get in is stuck in a field. Go figure."

In the act of swallowing, Alex choked. He pounded on his chest and coughed. Finally, eyes streaming, he turned back to the bar and squeaked out a response. "You're kidding me."

"It's not his fault. Little Bear Creek's at flood stage. Some of the roads are underwater."

While Alex had been coughing up apple cider and leaning against the wall, they had been joined by a middle-aged man of average height with a dark beard. He sprawled in one of the booths. He wore a shirt emblazoned with the logo of the airlines and his first name. Mike tossed him a bottle. Taking a ring of keys from his pocket, Al took a healthy swig. "Looks like you're gonna have to find yourself a ride, buddy. Soon as I finish my libation, I'm gonna put the airport to bed." He took another long swig and smacked his lips.

Alex tipped his head back against the wall. When he got his hands on his cousin…

"Did the plane to Detroit get out?" The woman two stools over swiveled around and addressed Al. Her brow furrowed as she waited for the response. Alex's dilemma was no concern of hers. *And they say New Yorkers are unfriendly.*

Al nodded. "Your brother made it out in the nick of time. They canceled the last flight in, so the airport's closing. What do you expect? There's a hurricane moving up the East Coast, and central Pennsylvania is on the outer edges. We get flooding. No big deal. Happens every spring."

"Good." Her stool scraped against the wooden floor as she stood and shrugged into the yellow poncho.

"What am I supposed to do?" Alex had the distinct feeling, of the four locals in the bar, the woman, Sera, was his best chance at finding a solution to his problem. But the guarded expression on her face as she paused—the bright vinyl puddled around her neck, emphasizing the blackness of the curly hair—had him rethinking his conclusion.

She pulled the poncho down, slipped her hands through the holes and shook her head, sending curls flying in all directions. "Where are you headed?"

Hope sparked in his chest. Maybe he had misjudged the woman. "Clover Hill Farms. Outside Bear Meadows."

"No kidding. Well, good luck." She picked up her paisley purse and headed for the door. "Thanks for the drink, Mike."

"Hey, Sera. Isn't Clover Hill Farms close to your place?" Scooby eyed Sera's glass with her unfinished drink. "You live right next—" Scooby's enthusiasm deflated at the woman's sharp glance.

One hand on the dark door, she paused. Her shoulders lifted and dropped, as if she had taken a big sigh. When she turned, his gaze met hers and held.

Pretty green eyes blinked once. She opened her mouth and then closed it again. A full minute passed before she replied. "I'm driving the pickup, Scooby. He doesn't look like a pickup kind of guy."

Alex knew if he didn't do something soon, he would be sleeping on the uncomfortable vinyl chairs in the lobby. So he smiled. For a brief second the woman smiled back, before the smile disappeared and her eyes became guarded. Up close, they almost appeared blue. If he didn't want to spend the night in the airport, the poncho-wearing, blue- or green-eyed woman was his last hope. "I could be a pickup kind of guy." He smiled in what he hoped was a persuasive manner. "I'll pay you."

She pursed her lips as she considered his answer. "Clover Hill Farms, huh?"

She caught the eye of the ticket agent. "There's no one left in the airport. What about the pilots?"

Al stroked his beard. "Gone."

Her chin dropped to her chest, as if in defeat. When she looked up, her jaw was set. "Show me your driver's license."

Alex supposed he shouldn't be surprised. In this day and age, a person couldn't be too careful. He pulled his wallet from his pocket, withdrew his New York license and laid it on the counter. She returned to the bar, every step hesitant as if this were the last place she wanted to be. She glanced down at the piece of plastic. "This license is expired." Despite the rain, or maybe because of it, her dark hair curled around her face.

Alex looked down at the piece of plastic. "What did you say?"

She tapped the plastic with one finger. "Your license is expired."

Alex looked around the bar at the three men. "Of course not." Picking up the license, he checked the date. She was right.

Somehow he had allowed the license to expire. Considering he didn't own a car, he supposed he shouldn't be surprised. He held the license in front of her eyes. "Look at the picture. Doesn't the picture look like me?"

"Not really. That guy has a beard."

He held the license out to the three men, and each shrugged. No question whose side they were on.

She eyed him warily. "Suppose you are Alexander Kimmel. So what? Kimmels don't own Clover Hill Farms." She tossed the license back onto the counter. "This doesn't exactly reassure me." Thrusting her shoulders back, she took a deep breath and stared the man straight in the eyes.

So she wasn't a trusting sort. He guessed that was a good thing. "I'm Cyrus Carter's cousin. My mother and his father are brother and sister. Call him. He's expecting me."

Her eyes narrowed as she looked Alex

up and down. "Why didn't Cy come pick you up?"

This time it was Alex's turn to shrug. "You got me. He said the new vet's coming over to look at a sick cow and he has to be there."

Finally the smile he had been trying for with the pickup response appeared on the woman's face. "Typical." A sharp wrinkle appeared between dark brows as she looked up at Alex. "You're Cy's cousin? For real?"

Mike slid a thin phone across the top of the bar. "Call him."

Sera picked up the cell phone and flipped through the screens. Finding what she needed, she held the phone to her ear. "Hello? Mrs. Carter? Hi. This is Serafina Callahan. Could I speak to Cyrus?" She nodded, her fingers toying with the snaps on her yellow poncho. "Yes, ma'am. We're fine. Listen—" She rolled her eyes and shot an irritated look in Alex's direction.

He held his hands out to the side.

"Good luck getting a word in edgewise." He smiled as he pictured his aunt pelting Sera with questions like snowballs.

Scooby picked up Sera's glass, and just as he lifted it to his lips, Mike snatched it out of his hand. "Sorry, buddy."

"Aww, come on. Just one sip." Scooby held up one finger.

"No." Mike emptied the glass in the sink with a smile.

"Mrs…Mrs. Carter, I'm at the airport, and there's a guy here who says he's Cy's cousin…Uh-huh…Uh-huh…He is? Well, what if…Uh-huh…I see…Thank you… Good night." She returned the phone to Mike, who dropped it in his shirt pocket.

Alex crossed his arms in satisfaction. "What did Aunt Jean say, Sera?" The satisfaction of being right bloomed in his chest. Now, if he could just convince her to give him a ride.

She stared at the bar. Her lips pursed once, twice, before she took a deep breath and looked at him, hard. "She confirmed you are who you say you are."

Sera's gaze flicked from the counter to his luggage. "That's all you brought?"

"I'm just here for the weekend. I have a flight home Monday morning." His license still lay on the counter. He retrieved it and returned his wallet to his back pocket.

"The New York connection. Out Monday, return Friday." Her lips pursed, then straightened, and pursed again, before settling into a slight grimace. She'd apparently arrived at a decision, because she sprang up and strode toward the dark door with the colorful glass. The yellow poncho flared around her jean-clad legs like a superhero's cape. "Come along, then."

Alex cast a glance first at Scooby, then the ticket agent and then Mike, who reached under the counter and pulled out a Hershey's bar, which he handed to Alex. "Try sweetening her up with this. She likes chocolate."

Scooby and Al followed Sera into the

main terminal. Switching off the lights in the bar, Mike disappeared into the back.

Grabbing his suitcase, Alex went to find the lady with the pickup. He wished he had never left the city.

CHAPTER TWO

As HE HEADED for the front doors, the big overhead lights dimmed, leaving the terminal lobby in shadows. The young woman in the yellow poncho was his only option. Despite the nagging feeling of uncertainty in his chest, he followed.

That quick, she had disappeared. The sidewalk and road in front of the terminal were empty. His cousin owed him big time after this. The least he could do when requesting a favor would be to pick him up at the airport. A sign read Taxi Stand, but the space was empty. Not unlike Scooby's car rental agency.

He was wondering if he should try to call Cy when a truck badly in need of a paint job jerked to a stop in front of him. Smoky exhaust poured out the back, blending with the rain. He looked around for a shiny pickup truck. But the parking area was dead.

The window rolled down. Serafina Callahan propped her elbow in the window. “You aren’t waiting for me to open the door for you, are you? Because that’s not part of the service.”

Alex continued to stare at the monstrosity. Silver duct tape rimmed the front wheel well. The original bed had been replaced with a wooden flatbed. “Is this thing safe?”

“Old Blue works just fine. She gets me where I’m going.” She rolled up her window, her shoulder rising and falling with each rotation of the handle.

Alex took a breath. He walked around the front of the truck and pulled open the passenger door. The floorboards were about three feet off the ground with no running board. He set his carry-on on the seat, grabbed the edge of the dash and jumped in. “I guess that’s all that counts.” The door screeched as he pulled it shut.

The lights over the main terminal door dimmed. Inside the ticket agent leaned against the glass doors and waved. "Interesting characters."

Sera shrugged. "What's your point?" She turned the truck out of the parking lot and onto the narrow road. The truck stalled in the middle of the two lanes.

Alarmed, Alex looked over his shoulder for oncoming traffic. "We're in the middle of the road."

"No kidding." Sera tried the key. The engine turned over once, twice, coughed, died.

"Do something." He was wishing more and more he had opted for the plastic seats in the lobby. At least he wouldn't be roadkill.

She switched off the headlights.

Alex pressed the heels of his hands to his eyes. He hadn't called his mother in three weeks. He would die without saying goodbye.

The engine turned over, coughed and caught. Sera flipped on the headlights and shifted into first gear. "You're a nervous sort, aren't you?"

Alex put his hand to his chest. "Only since I arrived here."

With the rain and the overcast sky, darkness had come early. The headlights lit up trees and shrubs close on both sides of the narrow road.

Looking for his phone, his hand felt the Hershey's bar in his coat pocket. Maybe she was low on sugar. He offered her the candy bar. "From Mike. He seems to think you like chocolate."

Her eyes lit on the bar held in his hand. She snatched the bar from his fingers. "And he would be right."

They both saw the tree branch in the middle of the road at the same time. She slammed on the brakes. His hand shot forward and gripped the dash.

"Sorry. Tree branch. Middle of the road." She ripped the paper from the candy bar and bit off a huge chunk. And then glanced his way guiltily. "I haven't eaten all day." She downshifted.

Except for the roaring of the big engine, the hiss of the tires on the wet road and the ripping of the candy bar wrapper, the next few miles passed in silence. The old truck seemed to find every pothole, which didn't help his headache one bit. Alex held on to an overhead handgrip as they bounced down the road in the dark. "There's no interstate highway between the airport and Clover Hill?"

In the glow of the dash lights, he thought he detected a small smile. "There is, but I don't think my truck will float. This way gives us the best chance of getting home without ending up in the Chesapeake." She cut him a quick glance. "Is that okay with you, Mr. Kimmel?"

"Call me—" His eyes widened as he saw the obstruction in the road while at the same time realizing she was looking at him. He opened his mouth to warn her but nothing came out. When she jerked her gaze back to the road, she twisted the wheel to one side, steering them toward a tree on the side of the road. Alex's head slammed sideways and bounced off the window.

He caught a brief glimpse of a white tail and a big tree as his hand again reached for the dash. He wasn't fast enough. His forehead hit the dash before his hand.

The engine rattled twice and then quit. Rain drummed on the roof of the cab. The headlights shone on a tangled mass of wet green. The tree they had been heading for was just outside the driver's-side window.

"You just had to devour that candy bar while driving in the middle of a monsoon." When he heard no response, his gaze slid from the tree to the driver, grimacing and rubbing her right knee. "Are you all right?" He looked her over for bleeding, but in the dim light provided by the headlights, he couldn't tell which dark spots were water and which were blood.

"Deer." She leaned her head back against the seat and shut her eyes.

"Deer?"

Opening her eyes, she said to him

slowly, "I thought they'd be bedded down in this rain."

"I see." He didn't see. All he cared about was whether they both survived the crash. Then, as he looked around, he cared even more about how they were getting out of this mess.

STARING AT THE blur of rain on the windshield, she was glad she was driving the sturdy, indestructible old pickup, because the tree would've done a lot more damage to a car than to the twenty-year-old truck. As far as her passenger... She glanced sideways. "I'm all right. Are you all right?"

The man rubbed his forehead. When he took his hand away, Sera saw a goose egg already forming above his right eyebrow. Leaning forward, she pressed her hand to his head.

As he jerked away, his head bounced off the window. "Ouch. This thing is a death trap." He pushed on the door, which gave a loud whine.

Sera leaned back against her door. The man wasn't very appreciative. "I was just trying to help."

He held up his hands. "You've done enough already, trust me."

She huffed out a blast of air. "Fine." She turned the key. The engine sputtered and died. She closed her eyes and muttered a quick prayer. She turned the key again. The engine ground over and over… *Please*... The engine caught and she breathed a sigh of relief. She would have to rock the truck out of the ditch. Alex could get in or get out. She gave up trying to be nice. He pulled the door shut just as she put the truck in first gear, pressed the throttle and then quickly moved the handle to Reverse. The truck rocked forward, then backward, then stalled. She tried twice more but with no luck. She looked at her companion and tried to adopt what she thought was a hopeful tone. Maybe she had been too harsh. "We're a little bit stuck."

"What was your first clue?" Alex

rubbed at the growing bump on his head before sending her a look. "So now what?"

Sera stared out at the branch pressed across the entire width of the windshield, blocking her view. Reddish buds were just pushing into leaf. The engine ticked in the silence.

She cleared her throat. "We walk."

Out of the corner of her eye she saw him turn to look at her, but her gaze remained on the windshield. "Can't you call a tow truck?" he asked.

She debated how to break the news to the newcomer. "I don't have a cell phone."

"You don't have..." His hand slapped his coat pocket. "I have a cell phone." He pulled his phone from his pocket and pressed a button. The interior of the cab lit up. He swiped the screen and waited. The light went out and the cab returned to darkness. "What the heck?"

Sera drummed her fingers on the steering wheel. If anyone was going to get them out of this dilemma, it was she. He was obviously totally dependent on technology. “Probably no signal.”

Alex looked from the phone to the woman and back again. “What do you mean, no signal?”

“I mean, there are no cell towers on this side of the valley.”

Mumbling under his breath, Alex shoved the phone back into his pocket. “This phone can do everything, he says. When I get my hands on that guy…”

The rain pounded a beat on the metal roof of the cab. Already the windows were steamed up. Sera waited until his mumbling faded before stating what she thought was the obvious. “I’ve got a bush on my side. Can you open your door? The sooner we start walking, the sooner we’re home.”

Alex pushed on the door with such force it slammed into the tree trunk they had just missed.

“Hey, you just dented my door.”

He gave her a steely-eyed glare. “How can you tell?”

"You might have a point." The man was getting cranky. And could she blame him? Maybe she should've shared the candy bar. At least then his sugar level would be up. She slid across the seat, where, although his feet were outside, he still leaned against the truck. "Excuse me, can you move? I can't get out."

Rather than move away, he turned, putting him much too close for comfort. Perching on the edge of the passenger seat, Sera waited for him to move away. Rain pattered the leaf-strewn ground around them. When his arms reached forward, she leaned back into the cab. His voice was gruff as he pulled up her hood. "It's raining out here. Can't have you getting wet."

His hands pulled the hood tight around her face. She took a deep breath to slow her heart rate. "I won't melt." Suddenly realizing his jacket had a hood as well, she reached over his shoulder to return the favor, which would have been fine if the truck weren't at a slight angle. When she reached forward, she started to slide off the seat, Alex automatically reached out to stop her fall. Her forward momentum, though, pushed Alex backward and they both landed in a patch of leaves with a soft splash. His arms wrapped around her waist, she lay motionless on top of him. “Are you okay?”

“Am I okay? Lady, ever since I met you it’s been one disaster after another. If you hadn’t—”

Not wanting to hear any more about the candy bar, she kissed him. And wonder of wonders, he finally stopped complaining. Which was all she wanted to do. So she kissed him again.

ALEX LAY IN the wet leaves. Suddenly the icy water trickling into his ears was of less consequence than what had just happened in the last few minutes. This woman, this monster-truck-driving woman who he had known for a grand total of two hours, had just kissed him. In the cold rain. With warm lips. He tightened his arms around her waist just as she pushed herself away. The only sound was rain pattering down. "What was that about?"

She stood and, gripping the edge of the truck bed, worked herself up onto safer ground. "Let's go, city boy. The sooner we start walking, the better."

He lay back and stared up into the tree. Raindrops splatted the middle of his forehead. Had he been dreaming? She acted as if nothing had happened. And that kiss was definitely not nothing.

Putting the confusing double negative to the back of his mind, he jumped up, retrieved his carry-on, and then slammed the truck door, the exertion only partially alleviating his annoyance. He was with a completely irrational woman. His Italian leather loafers squished through puddles as he gripped the sides of the truck bed to pull himself up onto the road. At her touch on his sleeve he wheeled around. "Where did you come from?"

Her brow furrowed. She pointed to the right. "Ready?" She took off down the road. Alex looked back at the truck, hopelessly mired in the muddy ditch. He could stay here and pray for a passing vehicle, or he could follow the country girl. Heavy trees and shrubs crowded the road on both sides. He hurried to catch up. "How far to your place?"

"Maybe two miles." The woman had quite a stride. She could give Manhattan pedestrians a run for their money. "So you live in the country, as well."

"Yep."

He wondered if she had taken offense. "I just meant like my cousin. Do you live on a farm?"

She stopped and faced him, poked his chest with her finger. "Look, I'm tired, I'm hungry and I don't feel like chitchat. Okay?"

"Fine. I was just making conversation." He continued on, lengthening his stride with determination. "But what was the deal with that kiss back there?"

Again with the finger in the chest. "First, I don't know what you're talking about. And second, we will never speak of this again."

Despite his best city-block-eating pace, she caught up, and they continued along the road until they left the thickest trees behind.

In the distance he saw a brief flicker. "Is that—" He squinted. "It is. Headlights. Maybe we can get a ride."

"They're going in the opposite direction."

"Aren't you the epitome of positive thinking? Are you telling me the locals won't stop for a couple of drowned rats in the middle of a monsoon?"

"I wouldn't. Look what happened to me. If I hadn't agreed to take you home—"

He stopped, indignant. "Me? You're blaming this on me? You're the one who took her eyes off the road to focus on a Hershey's bar."

Sera wheeled around. This time she gripped both shoulders with her hands and stood on her tiptoes. "Cool it with the Hershey's bar. I wouldn't have taken my eyes off the road..."

Nose to nose in the middle of the road, Alex had forgotten all about the oncoming vehicle until the headlights blinded him. But he could still see Sera's wet, white face, her dark, curly hair and lips, made red by her constant biting. He heard the whir of an automatic window and then a woman's voice. "Hey, you guys need a ride?"

Still absorbed in the stark color contrast of his companion's face, Alex was reluctant to answer. But of course, he had to. "I do. I mean, we do."

The side door of the van slid open. When he gripped Sera's arm to help her into the back seat, she shot him a look. Whether of surprise or consternation he couldn't tell in the dim light of the van. She climbed over a couple boxes and settled into a bucket seat.

The woman peeked over the front seat and reached out to shake hands. "Hi, I'm Wendy Valentine."

Alex shook her hand. "Thanks for stopping."

Sera leaned forward and also shook her hand. "Hey, you're the local weather girl, aren't you?"

With a sideways glance at the driver, Wendy laughed. "Up until last year I was. I'm on temporary assignment for an Atlanta station now." She punched the man in the shoulder. "Josh is my driver."

The look they shared and the ring on her left hand told Alex the young man with the dark beard was a lot more than her driver.

Peering into the rearview mirror, he spoke over his shoulder. "Josh Hunter. Where are you two headed?"

Sera responded before Alex could answer. "Not far. Last Chance Farm."

Irritated at her attempt to control the situation, Alex spoke up. "Actually, I'm headed to Clover Hill Farms."

Josh glanced over his shoulder. "You won't be getting to Clover Hill Farms tonight. We can get you to Last Chance

Farm, but the bridge over the creek is flooded. That's what we were doing, getting camera footage of the bridge for the local station." He executed a neat three-point turn and headed back in the direction from which he had come.

"Where's your vehicle? Were you in an accident?" Wendy's sharp eyes looked them over, presumably for signs of trauma.

"I… My truck ended up in a ditch." Her voice lowered to a mutter. "So much for doing a good deed."

"What did you say?" Alex looked at the woman huddled on the bucket seat, her feet propped on a suitcase on the floor. But he couldn't see her face since she was looking out the window.

"Nothing." Sera leaned forward. "There's a big white mailbox at the end of the lane. You can just drop us off there."

"I know where your farm is. Wendy's parents' house is a few miles farther down this road."

The vehicle slowed as Josh turned in

to the lane. Alex saw the white mailbox and then a long line of white board fence. A huge tree marked the end of the fence and then a big bush next to a small building. As Josh swung the vehicle around to the back of the big white house, the headlights lit up the earthen ramp leading to two big white barn doors. Swirling wisps of fog surrounded the cupola at the roof's peak.

Wendy gasped. "You have a bank barn. How beautiful. You know, you can't really see your place from the road." When the lights hit the white brick and blue shutters of the back of the house Wendy exclaimed again. "Gorgeous! When was your house built, Sera?"

"In 1855. We don't get much traffic out this way. Most people use the interstate."

Alex detected a note of pride in Sera's response. He slid open the side door. After dismounting, he turned and reached for Sera's hand to help her over the boxes. She hesitated.

"Now you're shy?" He felt a brief triumph as her cheeks pinked.

She took his hand but directed her comments to the couple in the front seat. "Thanks for the ride."

"You're welcome," Josh called out to them. The sliding door shut on its own, and Alex stood in the foggy mist with Sera, watching the van disappear down the drive.

"So the bridge over the creek is flooded and my cousin's place is on the other side." He turned and observed the big white barn building almost evaporating into the mist. "I can stay in the barn."

"Don't be ridiculous." She led the way to a trellis leading into a fenced-in yard. A cobblestone path extended to the back porch. Sera mounted the steps and pulled open the screen door. She pushed on the door with her shoulder, but it didn't budge.

Alex, reluctant to follow and still hoping his cousin would somehow miraculously appear, was only halfway down the path. He watched as she bumped the door with her hip. "Is it locked?"

She gave him a look as if she thought he wasn't very bright, then shook her head. "The door sticks when it rains." The third time she used her entire body to slam the door, which finally opened. Hand on the doorknob, she stopped, then looked back over her shoulder. "I should warn you. I have a dog. He's not fond of strangers."

Alex walked to the foot of the wooden steps and hesitated. He noticed her knit brow and turned-down lips and wondered what in the heck he was getting into. "Really."

She glanced away, avoiding his eyes. "Don't make any sudden moves around him, okay?"

He nodded, but the effort was lost. She was definitely avoiding his gaze. "What kind of dog?"

"Saint Bernard."

He pictured a big, stout animal with a

barrel fastened under his chin. "What's his name?"

Her eyes narrowed. Her lips twitched. "Cujo."

CHAPTER THREE

SERA DIDN'T USUALLY run in the rain, but the stranger currently occupying the bed in the spare room had thrown her. After a restless night and knowing a stranger slept under her roof, she needed to think. And the best place to think was outside. She stood on the porch and breathed deep of the chilly, damp air. Gray clouds hung low over the fields. She couldn't tell if the rain was over or if there was more to come.

"What do you think? Is it clearing up?" She glanced at her companion.

A tall, skinny mongrel with a coat the color of slate gazed up with concern. At the distant rumble of thunder, the dog turned and pressed his nose to the door. Of her two dogs, the animal who had appeared just the summer before was the more skittish one.

"The thunder's moving away, Lucky." But she opened the door and let him into the house, where he would disappear into the den and hide under the grand piano. Sera stretched and bounced down the stairs. She needed this run. It would relax her. She jogged through the arch and ran past the shed where she parked the truck. The empty space reminded her she had to figure out how to retrieve the old pickup from the ditch. The brushy branches of the big mock orange bush next to the building showed just a hint of green. Soon the shrub would be covered with thousands of snow-white blossoms and perfume the air with their sweet scent.

She ran past the field where tiny green shoots poked through the dark soil. Sweet corn was one of her most profitable crops. Few people grew their own, but most still loved the traditional sweet corn for summer picnics. She breathed deep of the damp air and continued her steady pace. She wondered if the newcomer was awake yet and how soon Cy Carter would arrive to claim his long-lost relative. Her breaths came shorter as she started up the incline to the top of the hill. Leaving the bare fields behind, she slowed and then stopped in the orchard. Fog shrouded the bare apple trees, but at least the rain had stopped. Usually at this point she could see Little Bear Creek, but fog hung so thick over the valley she couldn't see the bottom of the hill.

Heat rose up her neck and onto her cheeks as she remembered running off the road the night before. She should have been watching for deer, but the man's presence had distracted her. When she had slid across the seat to get out of the truck, he had reached up for her hood. But for a minute she thought he was standing there, hands up, waiting for her, as if he had lifted her down from the truck dozens of times. She had almost brushed away his outstretched arms. But the offer of help came so rarely she couldn't resist. Then when she had accidentally fallen against him and they lay there in the dark and the blessed quiet, she had the strangest urge to put her head on his chest and close her eyes. The surrounding darkness and the rain dropping on the leaves had created a kind of comfortable bubble that seemed made just for the two of them. Serafina Callahan and Alexander Kimmel. When he'd begun complaining, she just wanted him to stop talking. Just wanted one more minute of peace and quiet. So yes, she had kissed him. But if she pretended it hadn't happened…well, then, it hadn't happened. She shook her head to dispel the image.

The still-bare branches reached into the fog like bony fingers. Singling out a lone tree, she framed the shot with the thumbs and forefingers of both hands. She really should go back and get her camera. Funny that her brain still went into picture-taking mode after all this time. She took one last look at the foggy tableau and started back down the hill. The rain picked up.

Aunt Hope would have coffee brewing by now. And if she were lucky, their impromptu visitor would be out of the spare bedroom and across the creek where he belonged.

HE OPENED HIS eyes to Big Ben, the old-fashioned windup alarm clock his grandfather used to keep by the side of the bed. Next to the clock sat a crystal dish full of peppermints. He definitely wasn't sleeping in his own cramped bedroom on the Lower East Side. Rain drummed a steady rhythm on the roof. The bed was warm, and for a moment all he wanted to do was pull the comforter over his head and sink farther into the soft pillow that smelled like sunny days. The usual tenseness in his neck and shoulders was gone. Maybe he should put in for vacation. He wondered if he could actually relax for a week.

When he lifted his head off the pillow

to glance out the window, his forehead throbbed with pain. He probed the bump over his eye as he glanced around the spacious room. The white metal bed frame sat high off the floor, which was covered with a rag rug. Sheer curtains hung in the windows, but since the sun wasn't shining, the curtains had nothing to hide.

He lay back against the crisp pillowcase and closed his eyes. Thanks to the young couple with the van, he and Sera hadn't walked far the night before, but rolling around in the sodden leaves had left him wet and muddy. She had marched him through a dimly lit kitchen, down a dark hallway and up the stairs to the guest room and the bathroom, where he had taken a hot shower. He hadn't seen her since. He hadn't seen Cujo either, concluding the woman just wanted to mess with his head. She was doing a good job. His carry-on sat on a straight-back chair next to the window.

Throwing on a T-shirt and jeans, he entered the hallway and was greeted with the sight of six closed doors. He must have been more disoriented the night before than he realized, because he tried three doors, opening into empty bedrooms before finding the bathroom, where he splashed water on his face. His wet clothes from the night before still lay in the claw-foot tub. Then he descended the stairs into an entry. Gray light streamed through the side glass panels of the big front door, where a coatrack and bench sat to the right. He peeked through the adjacent doorway. A grand piano occupied the space between two windows at the front. A large rolltop desk occupied the other corner. In between, a couch fronted a brick fireplace.

He followed his nose down the hall toward the back of the house. Somebody had made coffee. Pictures covered almost every inch of the flowered wallpaper decorating the length of the hallway. Two baby pictures, a faded wedding photo, graduation pictures of a boy and a girl. He stopped and stared at a younger Sera. The dark hair was poker straight. A photograph of an orchard in bloom.

Leaving the old photos behind, he continued down the hall. The house was silent. His hostess was still asleep.

The coffee smell grew stronger as he entered the warm kitchen. The only light came from the flames glowing through the grates of an old white cookstove. Spying a coffeemaker on the counter, he touched the glass pot. Still warm.

He opened the overhead cupboard door and reached for a mug. Yellow script and a slipper-shaped yellow flower adorned opposite sides of a brown cup. *The Wildflower.*

"Coffee's not more than twenty minutes old."

At the sound of the unexpected voice, the cup flew out of his hands. Alex had always considered himself to have quick reflexes. He snagged the cup just before it hit the floor.

"Didn't mean to startle you."

Alex looked around the dim kitchen.

He still couldn't see where the voice had originated. The kitchen table in the middle of the room was unoccupied, a sugar bowl and salt and pepper shakers in the middle. In the corner opposite the cookstove was a rocking chair with an afghan, next to a lumpy dog pillow. At the sight, he stiffened. So there was a dog. Then he breathed a sigh of relief. The dog must be outside. He continued his perusal of the big kitchen. Sink, stove and refrigerator.

But when his investigation revealed a second dog pillow in the other corner occupied by a huge, spotted dog, his heart stopped. Snores came from the large wet nose, the lower lips quivering with each exhalation. The hairs on the back of Alex's neck prickled as he took in the size of the black, brown and white animal. *Cujo?*

Returning his gaze to the rocking chair, he squinted. A tiny woman sat there with an afghan over her lap. Her face was in shadows, which was why his gaze had skimmed past her the first time. "I'm sorry. I didn't see you." Keeping his voice low, he sneaked a glance at the big dog. Still asleep. "Do you mind if I have some coffee?"

"Help yourself." Her voice sounded hoarse. "So you're Jean's nephew from New York City."

Alex set his cup on the table. The chair scraped against the floor as he pulled it from the table. When the dog lifted his massive head to investigate, Alex froze. Only when the head dropped to the pillow did he breathe a sigh of relief and sit.

He sipped the hot, strong coffee before answering. "Yes, ma'am. Sorry for the imposition. I ran into Sera at the airport, she called my aunt and my aunt talked her into letting me stay here overnight. I guess the bridge was flooded."

"That's my Sera. Always taking in strays. In between all her other jobs."

Sipping the hot coffee, Alex's brows knit at the reference. "Are you Sera's grandmother?"

"I'm her great-aunt. You can call me Hope."

He glanced up at the rooster clock over the sink. He had slept later than usual. "Is Sera still sleeping?"

"Heavens, no. She runs every morning. Says it helps her organize her thoughts. You turning up must've given her something to think about." Chuckling, the woman stood. "Why don't I fix you some breakfast? Bacon and eggs sound good?" She laid the striped afghan over the back of the chair and smoothed the front of her blouse. Her gray hair was wrapped in a braid and pinned on top of her head.

Alex couldn't believe how tiny the woman was. Why, she barely reached his chest. "You shouldn't bother. Coffee's fine."

But the woman seemed not to have heard him as she retrieved a heavy black iron skillet and dropped it onto the wood stove with a clang. Minutes later bacon sizzled.

"So you're her great-aunt. Just the two of you here?"

She set a tub of butter and a jar of jam

in the middle of the table and paused to give him her undivided attention. "At the moment. Chance was just home for a visit. That's Sera's brother." Her face lit with a broad smile. "He's a singer. That's why she happened to be at the airport when you came in. Chance was on his way back to Nashville." She carried a carton of eggs to the stove. "Mark my words. One of these days he'll be singing at the Grand Ole Opry."

She cracked an egg into a smaller skillet with one hand. The sound seemed to finally stir the big dog, who stood and stretched. He took two steps in Alex's direction and growled, stared at him with droopy brown eyes.

"Should I leave?" He didn't take his eyes from the dog.

"Why do you ask?" She was busy at the stove, laying crispy strips of bacon on paper towels.

"Cujo's awake. Maybe I should go outside before he gets excited." Alex eased out of the chair and backed toward the door. The dog dropped his nose to the floor and snorted. Alex reached behind him for the door handle when he heard a footfall outside. The door slammed into him and sent him flying in the dog's direction. Coffee flew out of the cup as he tumbled onto the pillow where the big dog had been lying just seconds before. He curled up in a ball and waited, certain Cujo wouldn't appreciate a stranger in his bed. Cool air drifted over him from the open door.

"What are you doing?" Sera's voice was calm.

She probably didn't want to further excite the dog. Feeling a breeze, Alex peeked through the crook of his elbow. Inches from his face, a fluffy white tail waved back and forth. "Protecting my vital organs." When the tail continued to wag, he pushed himself upright and leaned against the wall. Pink tongue hanging out, the dog appeared to be smiling as he stared up at the young woman.

Alex was awestruck, his focus rooted

to the woman who'd pushed through the screen door. Her yellow hood was pushed back, revealing dark, curly hair caught up in a high ponytail. Black ringlets caressed her cheeks, pink from exertion.

Her face flushed and dripping water, Sera covered her mouth with her hand as she looked down at Alex. "Good idea. Quick thinking, in fact." She grabbed the dog on either side of the furry neck and spoke in a firm voice. "Cujo, not food. Not food. Outside." She opened the door and the dog trotted outside. "There, you're safe." At the same time a mottled gray dog about half the size of the Saint Bernard appeared from the hallway.

Alex wondered if he had just been made a fool of but decided as long as the monster dog was outside he didn't care. The gray dog appeared harmless. Rising from the pillow, he eyed the coffee leaving a dark stripe down the flowered wallpaper. "Sorry about your wall."

Pulling two towels from a drawer, Sera handed him one and then, wiping her face with the other, moved to the stove to exchange a few quiet words with her great-aunt. Alex thought he heard a chuckle from the older woman, but it may have been a cough. He wiped the spilled coffee first from the wall and then the floor.

"Here you go, young man." A big smile on her face, the older woman set a plate where he had been sitting before the dog woke up.

Three eggs and at least six strips of bacon. "I don't usually eat this much for breakfast." He glanced at the older woman, who still wore the wide smile. He could only guess she was happy to have someone to cook for.

With a chuckle she refilled his cup. "You're a growing boy. Eat up, son." She glanced behind him. "You deserve it after the morning you've had."

Just as he lifted his cup to his lips, the gray dog stuck his nose between his elbow and his waist, jiggling the full cup. "Ouch." Hot coffee soaked through his clean jeans. He grabbed the towel and pressed it to his thigh.

Sera rushed over and grabbed the dog by the collar. Meeting his gaze for just a second, she smiled. "Lucky, stop that." Sera coaxed the dog to the pillow by the rocking chair, where Lucky rested his head on his paws, dark eyes darting between the woman and the man.

Sera pulled the yellow poncho over her head and hung it on a hook behind the door. "Maybe we should get you a travel mug, Mr. Kimmel. You're having serious coffee issues this morning."

Alex looked around the big kitchen for more pillows. Just the two. Biting off half a piece of bacon, he threw Sera a long look. "Have I met all your animals?"

Before answering, Sera poured a cup of coffee and then turned and leaned against the counter. "You've met both of my dogs, but not all of my animals." She brought the cup to her lips. "Did you sleep well?"

He swore her eyes—he couldn't decide if they were blue or green—had twinkled, and he feared she had something else up her sleeve. He refused to give her the satisfaction of showing his concern. "Like the proverbial log. Is the bridge still flooded?"

"Too foggy to see." She grabbed the last piece of bacon from his plate and sat opposite him.

He scowled at his plate. "I should call Cy. I have a lot of work to do. The sooner he can pick me up, the easier for everyone."

"Work? I thought you were visiting your relatives."

He decided to ignore the comment. Pulling his phone from his pants pocket, he pressed a button. Nothing. He stood and walked over to the window above the sink. Then he turned an eye on Sera. "Don't tell me. No cell towers around here."

"Oh, we have cell towers." She crossed her legs and smoothed the fabric of her sweatpants as if she were wearing linen trousers.

Holding the phone closer to the window, he tried again. Still nothing. He fixed her with a stare.

Holding the cup to her lips, she shrugged. "But we're in a bit of a dip here. If you want a signal for your cell phone, you'll have to walk up to the orchard on the hill." She gulped her coffee and sighed, as if her job were done.

Clenching his fingers around the cell, he glanced down at the screen, which displayed a photo of the Brooklyn Bridge. Somewhere he wished he were at the moment. Anywhere, as a matter of fact. The Golden Gate Bridge would do, as well. Any bridge. "So no contact with the outside world."

"Don't be ridiculous." Sera walked over to the back door and held out both hands like a model on a game show. A phone hung between the door frame and the cupboard. She picked up the receiver. "You've heard of landlines, I presume." She dialed a number.

Alex walked back down the hall,

leaving Sera to make arrangements for someone to pick him up. If he stayed in the kitchen one minute longer with the monster-truck-driving madam, he feared he might rip the phone out of the wall in frustration. And then she would sic the dogs on him and he would be history. He stared out through the glass panels flanking the front door to the lane they had driven down the night before. For the first time, he noticed two horses in the front pasture. They would probably turn on him as well, stomping him into pieces in the dirt.

"Alex. Your cousin wants to talk to you." Turning away from the grazing animals, he looked down the dark hall. Sera's head peeked around the corner. She held out the handset, connected to the wall with a curly cord.

He walked back past the photos and took the receiver from her hand. "Hello?"

"Hey, cuz. How was your night?" Cyrus's deep voice echoed through the phone. If Alex didn't know better, he could swear his cousin sounded amused.

Turning his back to the kitchen, Alex stretched the cord into the hallway. "Listen, whatever this favor is, it better be quick. You've already used up most of your quota. She wrecked the truck last night. Among other things. I'm lucky to be alive."

Cyrus laughed. "Where's the truck?"

Alex held out the phone and looked at the receiver, unable to believe his cousin's question. "Where's the truck? How about, am I hurt?"

"Obviously you're not hurt, or we wouldn't be talking. Where's the truck?"

"Not far from here. You'll pass it when you come to pick me up."

"Well, that's the thing. See, the bridge is still flooded, and I can't come get you unless I go way out of my way. Unfortunately, I don't have the time."

Alex smacked the wall with his fist and then winced at the pain. "I wanted to stay in a hotel in Shadow Falls in the first place, but you insisted I—"

"Whoa, fella. Settle down. By staying at Sera's—I already asked Sera if you could stay another night and of course, being the nice person she is, she said yes—you can do me a favor while you're there."

Summoning what patience he had left, Alex was reminded that Cyrus was indeed Jean's son. The two could talk your ear off. Funny how easily his cousin had slipped in the news he wasn't coming to get him. "You're the one who suggested I stay with you while I'm working on the theater mall project. You said we could get reacquainted."

"I did. I do. And we will. But I want you to look over Sera's farm and give me a fair market value. So this little twist of circumstances works to my advantage."

Alex turned. Sera stood at the back door, hands behind her in the pockets of her jeans, her hair curling as it dried. He lowered his voice. "She's selling you her farm?"

"She is. She just doesn't know it yet. One way or the other, Last Chance Farm is going to be mine by the end of the year. And you, my favorite cousin from the big city, are going to help make that happen."

CHAPTER FOUR

SHE STOOD ON the back porch, breathing in the damp air and waiting while Aunt Hope found Alex a pair of Chance's rubber boots and a poncho. She had absolutely no desire to show their visitor around the farm, but when he had asked, and Aunt Hope said, "Why, that's a good idea, gives me some quiet time," she didn't have much choice.

Underneath the kitchen window, Aunt Hope's herb garden sported bright green sprouts in the freshly turned earth despite the cool spring. She would package herb bouquets for the farmer's market along with Sera's larger produce. The onion sets she had planted two months earlier, just before the onion snow—hopefully the last snow of winter—had sprouted.

A clump of chives in the corner grew green, and a double row of string for the sugar snap peas ran along the edge. On the trellis, new leaves jutted from the rose canes woven through the lattice. The door opened behind her.

The heavy air seemed to shift as he came to stand beside her. She moved an inch to the left. "Where would you like to go?"

"I don't know. I got the feeling your great-aunt wanted us out of the house, so here I am. I don't want to keep you from your work."

She shrugged. "Actually, with the rain, there's not much to do today. The soil's too wet to work." She finally turned to look at him. Light brown stubble, a shade lighter than his hair, covered his face.

"Where's Cujo?" He scanned the enclosed yard and then the open space between the backyard and the barn.

Fighting back a smile, she cleared her throat and tried to sound serious. "Don't worry. He has a morning routine. He won't bother you." She noticed Alex shivered, but whether from the damp chill or her words, she couldn't say. "Let's go." She strode off in the direction of the barn.

The fog swirled around them as she led Alex past the shed and the big mock orange bush. Just beyond the garden, the white barn loomed out of the fog. Sera opened a door fitted into the gray stone foundation and entered the dim interior. When Alex didn't follow, she stuck her head out the door.

Alex stared up at the huge structure.

"Committing the dimensions to memory?"

"No. Just looking." With a last glance at the barn, he followed her inside.

Sera flicked a switch and a row of light bulbs illuminated a long hallway with stalls on one side and an open stairway on the other. "We're on the lower floor of a bank barn. Built the year after the house."

Alex peeked into the nearest stall. "Do you have any animals?"

"Two old horses. Mine and my mom's. Sometimes I put them in during the winter, if the weather's bad."

"That's right. I saw a bay and a palomino out front."

"That's them. And as of yesterday we have a litter of kittens." She dropped to her knees on a pile of hay under a short flight of simple wooden stairs. She pulled aside the hay to show Alex five tiger-striped kittens and one black, mewing and crawling, their eyes still closed. "People drop animals off down by the mailbox. Sometimes dogs but mostly cats. I usually take them to the animal shelter, but this one had her kittens before I could get around to it. Six kittens. Can you believe it?"

"You have a lot of room. What's six more cats?" Alex leaned against the stairs and crossed his arms.

He was obviously bored. Sera reached into a container and emptied food into a metal pan. "If the mama cat isn't fixed, she could have two more litters this year.

And these kittens could be having kittens by September. Trust me, it gets expensive."

"Where's the mother?"

"She's out earning her keep."

Alex threw her a puzzled look. "Excuse me?"

Relaxing on her knees, bent over the kittens, Sera smiled. "Catching mice, I hope. Everybody has a job on the farm."

"I see."

Sera pushed the bedding back around the litter and stood, brushing bits of hay from her sweatpants.

"Two dogs, two horses and seven cats."

She nodded. "Eight cats. Smoky is a gray tomcat and he's neutered. But I can't afford to spay or neuter every cat that's dropped off. Hazards of owning a farm."

When he didn't answer, she fastened the lid on the cat-food container. "I'll show you where we used to store the hay." She started up the stairs and disappeared. Her head reappeared through the hole cut in the ceiling. "Be careful. These are just boards nailed on risers."

Gripping the edge of the upper floor, Alex climbed the stairs and poked his head through the hole. He pulled himself out into the upstairs. "This place is huge."

She brushed some hay off a wide beam running across the width of the barn. "Chance and I used to play hide-and-seek in here with Cy and his older sister all the time." She looked up at a fluttering of wings high in the loft. "We would play for hours."

Walking to the big open barn doors, Alex stood at the top of the earthen ramp that led down to the car shed and looked out across the fields, where tiny green shoots poked through the soil. "Corn?"

Nodding, she came to stand beside him. "Sweet corn."

"So you and Cy are old friends?"

She started at the shift in conversation. The man seemed too inquisitive for someone just passing through, but then again maybe he was just making small talk. "We've known each other for a long time." She hesitated, then continued, "Funny, you and I have never crossed paths."

He took so long to answer she thought he hadn't heard her. His response was quiet. "My parents moved to Shadow Falls after I was in college. Cy and I didn't spend much time together as kids."

She sighed. "He wants to buy the place." She thought Alex would look surprised, but he just continued to stare out at the fields.

As a bird swooped by them out the doors, he glanced up at the rafters. "Is the farm for sale?"

She bit her lip. "Good question."

He finally fixed her with the same studied stare he had been bestowing on the fields. "How about that tour?"

"Follow me. You'll want to ride." She led the way to the empty shed.

"Are you driving?"

One raised light brown eyebrow hinted at Sera landing in the ditch the night before. She propped her hands on her hips. "Of course."

The golf cart was parked in the third stall. The empty middle stall reminded her again she had to figure out a way to retrieve the truck. Settling into the front seat, Sera waited for Alex. But only when she patted the seat beside her did Alex move toward the vehicle.

"A golf cart. On a farm?"

She turned the key. "My dad would take any payment for a gig. He and the band did a show at a golf course fund-raiser one year."

Alex reached for the back of the seat and then froze. "Wait a minute. I thought you said he wasn't around."

Sera looked over her shoulder. The Saint Bernard lay curled up in the wooden bed of the golf cart. She threw Alex a glance. "I said he had things to do. A ride around the property is one of them. He's too lazy to walk."

With a last narrow-eyed glance at the dog, Alex settled next to her and gripped the edge of his seat. "I think I'm ready." He pulled out his phone, checked the time and with a grimace returned the phone to his pocket.

"Got somewhere to be?" Sera frowned as she pulled out of the shed. This guy wasn't interested in looking around. At that moment she decided to let Cy know in no uncertain terms how much he owed her for babysitting his cousin. "We'll start out front."

Sera pointed to the fields on either side of the lane leading to the house. "Horse pasture. Just my mom's horse and mine now."

"Very nice." Alex let go of the dash and leaned back in the seat. "Do you ride?"

A feeling of nostalgia washed over her as they passed the two horses. At one time she had ridden her palomino gelding every day. "Not as much as I used to. You?"

Alex shook his head. "The few times we visited, Cy and I would ride his ponies down to the creek. But it's been a long time."

At the mailbox Sera turned left onto the berm of the main road but soon opted for a tight rutted two track that took them into a patch of woods.

The golf cart bounced over a fallen branch. At his grunt she gave him an appraising look. "How's your head?"

"Not bad. Your great-aunt's coffee helped quite a bit." He glanced around. "Lots of trees."

"We have twenty acres of timber. It might be ready to be logged. That'll give me some extra cash."

"Is money tight?" Alex didn't look at her when he asked the question, just held on to the dash and scrutinized his surroundings as she motored through the woods.

At his question a tingle ran down her spine as she remembered who she was talking to. Cy's cousin. Cy Carter, the neighbor who had indicated his interest in buying her family's farm. "Just something we do periodically."

Leaving the woods behind, she followed the narrow path uphill until they came out among the bare trees of the apple orchard. She shut off the golf cart and leaned back against the seat. "Your cousin has a flag—"

"Finally I have a signal. I have to make a call." He jumped out of the cart and strode off.

"Okay." But her reply was wasted. He was already walking away, talking rapidly and gesticulating in the air. *Why exactly was this New York cousin visiting his country relative?* Soon enough, he would be out of her hair.

His face was pensive as he walked back to the cart. He shoved the phone in his pocket, glanced briefly at the Saint Bernard and resumed his place next to her. He drummed his fingers on his thigh. "Does the quiet ever get on your nerves?"

"You get used to it."

He gestured at the trees around them. "What kind of trees?"

"Apple."

Alex's brows raised in surprise. "All of them?"

"Yep." She nodded. "These apples are eating apples. Crisp, sweet. They ripen early September. I sell them at the farmer's market in town." She pointed to the low cloud cover hanging over the creek. "Your cousin's place is on the other side."

"What about that place?" He pointed to a small log cabin at the base of the hill next to another grove of trees. Smoke coming out the stone chimney disappeared into the fog.

"That's the oldest structure on the farm." She followed his gaze, thinking of the older man inside recovering from pneumonia. With a stab of guilt, she remembered the flue should have been checked last year and she hadn't had the money to hire someone. This year, for sure.

In the sudden silence a moan sounded

from the cart bed. They both looked over their shoulders at the big dog.

Alex's left eyebrow lifted so high it disappeared under a shock of hair. "Was that a growl or a groan?"

Sera shrugged and frowned, pretending to be concerned. "You just never know with him. Ready to head back?"

"Sure." He pointed to the trees next to the small cabin. "Are they apple trees, as well?"

"Yes, but they're not the best. Sometimes Aunt Hope makes apple crisp, but I don't know what my mom was thinking when she planted them. She always said how great the soil up here was for apples, but I just don't get it. I can't give them away." She turned the cart around and headed back toward the house.

"So you and your great-aunt own the farm."

Sera peered at Alex, wondering why he was asking so many questions, but he was looking around at the orchard. "My brother and I do. Aunt Hope will live here as long as…as long as we do."

"But your brother lives in Nashville."

How did he know that? "True." He had been alone in the kitchen with Aunt Hope, and Aunt Hope trusted everybody.

"So where do your parents live?"

As always, the question caused her heart to stutter. After ten years, she thought the response would get easier. But it never did. "They passed away." Out of the corner of her eye she saw Alex glance her way. She pulled up to the arch leading into the backyard, grateful he had waited until the tour was over to bring up the subject of her parents. "Here you are. You should go on in." She waited until he stepped out, and without a backward glance, she and the Saint Bernard went for another ride. Being outside in the fog and the rain was still better than being inside with the inquisitive stranger.

ALEX AGAIN WOKE to silence Sunday morning. The thick fog had hovered over the area all day. Except for supper, Sera had kept out of sight. While Aunt Hope napped after lunch, he sat at the rolltop in the front room. The desk surface was covered with stacks of papers as was the floor between the chair and the bookcase. The amount of dust told him the stacks hadn't been disturbed in years. He spent a few hours working on the theater mall complex planned for the local area, then found an old paperback and spent the rest of the day reading.

Now he lay still in the comfortable bed. No rain drumming on the roof, no water running through the drainpipe at the side of the house. He glanced at the window by the bed. Faint light shone through the gauze curtains.

He lay in the soft bed thinking about his cousin's comment. After Sera's tour the day before, he wasn't surprised Cy wanted the farm. Though the house and barn both were in serious need of maintenance, the structures were solid. And the property was fine. If just Sera and her great-aunt lived here, no wonder they couldn't keep up. He was surprised she hadn't sold long ago. Alex wasn't shocked that Cyrus wanted to expand his operation. One thing he and his cousin had in common was a desire to outdo their fathers. Of course Cy would be interested in Last Chance Farm.

The clothes he had worn on the flight in two days ago were pressed and folded neatly on top of the dresser. Aunt Hope could give his laundry service a run for its money. His loafers, placed near the cookstove the day before, had finally dried but would never be the same.

"But they'll get me home." Alex stretched. Despite the fog yesterday, he had enjoyed riding around the farm with Sera in the golf cart. After brushing his teeth and combing his hair, he dressed and grabbed his overnight bag.

He strolled down the stairs and cast a last glance over the pictures in the hallway before entering the kitchen. The room was empty, but the light on the coffee maker was lit. He opened the cupboard and removed the mug with the yellow script. He set his bag by the back door and helped himself to coffee.

The two dog pillows were empty, as was the rocking chair. He strolled over to the sink, where a beam of light lit the purple and pink blossoms of the African violets. Through the window he saw Sera's truck parked next to the barn and wondered how she had recovered it. He walked outside, keeping an eye out for the dangerous Saint Bernard.

He approached the truck. The bed was filled with firewood. Seeing no signs of life other than a tiger-striped cat, presumably the culprit who had chosen this farm for a home for her and her kittens, skulking through the herb garden, he decided to walk up to the orchard and make a phone call.

From the top of the hill, he could see the stream below, winding its way between the fields of corn and grass. Beyond the bare trees he could make out the silver tops of Cyrus's grain silos, an American flag at the top of the tallest was the only bit of color in the landscape.

After a quick call to the airport and some schedule changes, he punched a familiar number. "Good morning."

"Alex?" The phone sounded as if it had been dropped.

He looked at the receiver to see if he had hit the right number and then hit the speaker button. "Carrie? Are you there?"

"Alex? Hold on." Carrie Oliver must have gone outside because Alex heard the sound of a door closing. Daughter of the founder of Oliver and Associates, Carrie was one of his two closest friends from law school. She had been instrumental in bringing him into her father's firm. "Hi. You're up early."

"So are you." Alex looked at the surrounding trees, picturing the sidewalk and steps outside Carrie's apartment. "Where are you?"

"Helping Will." Through the phone, the

sound of a siren whooped nearby, then faded.

"Helping Will do what?" Will was the other close friend from law school, except Will had lasted only a year before dropping out. With the chirping of the birds and the wind rustling the leaves in the trees, Alex felt very far away from Manhattan. "Is he there? With you?"

"Actually," Carrie said, chuckling, "I'm with him. He's rearranging the seating area outside the bar, getting ready for a rush of customers. Springtime in New York, you know." A backup alarm beeped. "What are you doing?"

"You wouldn't believe it if I told you." He waited for her response.

"Did you visit your parents yet?"

Alex looked up at the blue sky. Of course Carrie would assume he would see his parents while working in the area. "No, there was a lot of rain here that caused flooding. I didn't get to see them yet. Long story."

"Oh. Listen, I better go see if Will

needs any more help. Did you look at the property yet?"

"No. Like I said, it's complicated." He didn't bother to tell her the weekend had been wasted. "Tell Will I said hello."

"Okay. Bye, Alex."

"Bye." Alex slipped the phone into his shirt pocket and started back down the hill. Carrie and he had been splitting the theater mall complexes. If not for his familiarity with the area and the fact that his relatives lived close by, she would be the one from Oliver and Associates on this trip.

"NICE TRUCK." Sera eyed the late-model extended-cab pickup her neighbor parked by the back door. "Really green." The paint seemed to sparkle in the afternoon sun.

With his long legs, the tall man didn't have any trouble exiting the truck. "Thanks. Owner had to sell it quick. I couldn't pass up the deal." He leaned against the truck and crossed his massive arms. He crinkled his eyes. "So what have you done with my cousin? Do you have him plowing the back forty?"

"He's probably still asleep."

"He's a New Yorker. I'd expect him to be up and around." Cyrus's face broke into a broad smile as he looked over her shoulder.

Sera turned. Alex approached them with a matching smile and an outstretched hand. "About time you showed up."

"Hey, buddy, did Sera make you sleep in the barn?" Cyrus gripped his shoulder in a one-armed hug.

"Apparently the only cell reception is up at the orchard." He looked at Sera for the first time. "How did you get your truck back?"

Sera inclined her head toward Cyrus. "Your cousin and his heavy equipment." When she saw the Saint Bernard appear from behind the mock orange bush, she whistled.

"It's the least I could do with her having to put up with you all weekend." He punched Alex in the shoulder, then knelt and threw an arm around the dog's neck. "Hey, Rocky, how are you, old fella?" He ruffled the fluffy ears.

The dog growled.

Sera felt more than saw Alex's head as it swiveled in her direction. Knowing his eyes would be accusatory, she kept her gaze lowered.

"Rocky?" Alex sputtered. "I thought you said his name was Cujo."

Busy inspecting her fingernails, Sera shrugged.

"She told you his name was Cujo?" Cyrus threw back his head with a laugh. His shoulders continued to shake as he stood and leaned against the truck.

Alex came forward. "I should get my bag."

"Your bag's on the porch." Sera clenched her hands, wondering at the sudden trembling in her fingers.

"Then I should say goodbye to Aunt Hope."

"She's at church." The sooner he was

gone, the sooner things would return to normal.

"Tell her I said thanks for everything." He reached out his hand.

She stared at the long fingers, the buffed nails. She reached out, shook his hand and then withdrew hers as if she had touched a hot skillet. "I will."

"Listen, Sera, there's something you should know." Cyrus had sobered and glanced from her to Alex and back again.

"Let's just go, Cy." Alex tugged on his cousin's arm.

Cyrus brushed him off. "I didn't plan on Alex staying here. The bridge flooded and you were at the airport, so that was a coincidence."

Sera looked from one man to the other, wondering why Alex seemed so uncomfortable and Cyrus so serious. "Giving him a ride was no problem, Cy. And thanks again for bringing my truck back. And the firewood."

Cy inclined his head. "You're welcome.

Glad to help. I don't know if he mentioned it, but Alex is an attorney."

"Oh, really?" Her eyes narrowed just a fraction as she glanced his way. "Gee, my favorite type of person."

"He's a real estate attorney, Sera. He handles large-scale property acquisitions. Right now he's got a company wanting to put in theater mall complexes in rural areas. He knows the going rate for farm property better than anybody."

"Terrific." She stared at Cy, then Alex. She could hear the beat of her heart thumping in her ears. "Oh, I get it. This is part of your plan to force me into selling."

"Better me than the bank, Sera."

She propped her fists on her hips, suddenly aware she, and the farm, were a topic of conversation. "What do you know about my finances?"

"Everybody knows." His face looked solemn.

She looked then at Alex, whose face had turned pale. "Aren't you the clever cousin? Pretending to be stranded and then tricking my great-aunt and me into giving you a tour of the property."

"That's not why—"

She spun on her heel and headed for the house. "Get off my property, both of you."

CHAPTER FIVE

"YOU COULDN'T THINK of an easier way to let her know I'm an attorney?" Alex sat in the passenger seat of his cousin's truck on their way back to the airport. Instead of waiting for the direct Monday flight, he was so eager to return to the city he had opted for a Sunday afternoon return via Detroit. Anything to get back to normal. "Now she's mad. How does that help your case?"

"She'll get over it. What choice does she have? Whether she likes it or not, she needs me." Cyrus pressed a button in the middle of the truck console. "Want your seat warmer on?"

"No, I don't want my seat warmer on." Alex ran a hand over the soft leather seat. "That's your plan? She needs you? She seemed kind of surprised. Have you even made an offer?"

"She and her great-aunt came over to the house New Year's Day for pork and sauerkraut. I brought up the subject then and asked her to think about it. I understand the great-aunt is no longer on the deed." He ran a hand through curly reddish-brown hair.

"And you haven't spoken since?"

"No." He shrugged. "Dad has suddenly decided to retire. He spends all his time working on some project in the basement, so I've been busier than a bee in a clover patch."

"You realize she hasn't yet made up her mind."

"I told you, cuz. One way or the other, Sera's farm is destined to be absorbed." He tilted his head and spoke out of one corner of his mouth. "By me. I tell you, buddy, when I set my sights on something—" he slapped the leather-wrapped steering wheel for added emphasis "—I get it."

"Why her farm? Why not the farm on the other side of yours?"

"As a matter of fact, I am in the process of buying the farm on my other side. Sera's farm borders the creek. If I own her farm, I own both sides of the creek. Water on the property is a good thing, city boy. Besides, she barely has two nickels to rub together."

"Would you keep the orchard?"

Cyrus drew his forefinger across his throat with a smile.

Alex looked out the window at the passing scenery. Plowed fields stretched on either side to the base of the ridges lining the wide valley. Cy's intention to destroy the apple orchard made him oddly sad. When he turned to ask the man a question, he suddenly realized his cousin was more dressed up than usual. "You didn't have to dress up to take me to the airport."

Cyrus slanted a look in Alex's direction and smiled. "I'm taking the vet out for dinner later."

Alex wondered what the smile was about. "He's probably used to seeing you in your work clothes. And you—" he sniffed and caught the odor of cologne "—smell good."

"She—" Cyrus stressed the pronoun "—is used to seeing me in my work clothes. I thought I'd show her another side to Cyrus Carter."

"She?" Alex stared out the side window and wondered at the queasiness in his stomach. Was he uncomfortable with the idea of his aggressive cousin steamrollering the lovely Sera and her elderly great-aunt? After all, Cy was just trying to grow his business. Maybe the queasiness was just hunger, because he hardly knew the woman. "Sera was pretty mad at you. Maybe you should take her some candy. She likes chocolate."

Cy tilted his head and wrinkled his brow. "How do you know?"

"I pay attention to detail."

"So this is a catch-more-flies-with-honey-than-vinegar kind of approach." Cy chuckled.

"Assuming you want flies." Alex glimpsed an airport sign pointing to the right. "Hey, you missed the airport exit."

With his gaze locked on the road ahead, Cyrus didn't answer.

Alex waited, at first thinking Cyrus had a shortcut. But when he saw the sign announcing the outskirts of Shadow Falls, he knew. "No. Cyrus, you're not." He leaned forward and peered out the window at familiar streets. "I don't have time to stop at the house."

Cyrus threw him a glance. "You do and we are. Your mom had dinner planned for last night and, well, you know what happened there, so I promised her we'd come by for lunch."

"I'll miss my flight." Alex gripped the door handle, as if by so doing he could stop the truck from driving up to his parents' home.

"I called Al and asked him to switch you to a later flight. And since today's flight isn't direct, I thought you might even want to wait until morning to go back." Cyrus slowed as he pulled in between two brick pillars. "Gives you more time to spend with your parents."

Nestled among a stand of pines, the ranch house sat back on a long expanse of manicured lawn. Moving to Shadow Falls and building the new house after Alex had left for college, Alex's father had purchased two lots, allowing plenty of green space around the brown brick home. Cyrus parked in front of the two-car garage and turned off the engine.

Neither man made a move to get out of the truck. "This isn't a good idea." Alex stared up at the basketball hoop over the garage door, marveling how the object of many hours of play was still in place.

"It's been years since you turned down your dad's offer for the job with him and took the one in New York. He's over it by now. Isn't he?"

Alex snorted and shook his head. "If

it's not one thing, it's another. There's no pleasing the man."

"I can't speak for your dad, but I know your mom misses you. My mom told me. They talk a lot."

Alex nodded. His mother and Cy's had always been close. "Let's get this over with."

He walked around the truck. Dark green rhododendron bushes crowded the long front porch. The buds were about to burst with what Alex knew would be pink blossoms. The shrubs were bigger than he remembered, as were the pine trees. But then, he hadn't been back for a while. He marched up the front steps and knocked on the door. When he heard no movement from inside the house, he knocked again. By this time, Cyrus stood behind him. "Why don't you go in? This is your home."

Alex reached for the door handle just as the large oak door swung open. His father stood in the opening, his thick hair whiter than Alex recalled. But the tall man stood as straight as ever, his shoulders thrown back as if he were at attention.

Max Kimmel looked his son up and down. "So, the prodigal's returned. Hope you're not here to throw me and your mother out of our home." Leaving the door open, he turned and walked away, throwing his final retort over his shoulder. "Because I'd wish you luck with that."

"SOMETHING SMELLS GOOD." Entering the kitchen, Aunt Hope turned back at the door and waved. "Bernie and Babs Valentine brought me home today." She set her black purse on the bench by the door and untied the scarf around her hair. "They live just up the road, you know."

Sera pulled a pan of corn bread out of the oven and set it on the counter to cool. Stirring the chili on the stove, she smiled at her great-aunt. "So I heard. Their daughter Wendy gave us a ride home the other night. She's beautiful. And so accomplished. She's traveling the country doing interviews for an Atlanta station. How cool is that?"

"She's no more beautiful than you, dear." Aunt Hope squeezed her arm as she passed by on her way to the refrigerator. "And you could've done that, too, if things had been different."

Though ten years had passed, her stomach still dropped whenever she thought of her missed opportunities. "Are you ready for lunch?"

"I'm starving." Hope set the butter dish in the middle of the table, then pulled silverware from the drawer. She paused. "Is Alex still here?"

Sera shook her head. "Cyrus picked him up this morning." Heat rose to her cheeks as she thought of the deception by the cousins, but she saw no need to worry Aunt Hope. "Cyrus got a new truck. It's bright green."

Hope clucked and shook her head. "That boy always did like the finer things. Being a farmer, you'd think he'd remember to put away for the lean times. You just never know."

Lean times, indeed. After setting their chili on the table, Sera cut two squares of corn bread and brought them over, as well. Glancing at her great-aunt, she decided the time had come. She took her seat and waited until her great-aunt had spread butter over the corn bread. "You know, Cyrus is doing pretty well since he took over his dad's farm."

"I'm sure he is. After all, he went to college for that. But sometimes the best way to learn is through the school of hard knocks. Cyrus has always had things easy. His father handed the farm to him free and clear. Lucky for him, his sister wanted nothing to do with farming."

"He wants to be the biggest dairy farm on the East Coast."

"I'm not surprised." Spooning chili into her mouth, Hope threw her a look. "Did you use our tomatoes in this recipe?"

"Of course." If they had produce to can, they had less to buy at the store.

Hope dabbed her lips with a paper napkin. “I thought so. Wouldn’t be as good otherwise.”

“Anyway, about Cyrus…he said he needs more land.” New Year’s Day, Cyrus had cornered her in the hallway and brought the subject up. She had yet to give him an answer. But with summer just around the corner, she knew he was anxious for a decision. That’s why she had waited this long to tell Aunt Hope what she was planning.

“He’s already renting our fields. Can’t he rent from someone else?”

“He wants to buy our farm.”

At her words, Hope straightened. Sera couldn’t meet her gaze. Instead, she finished the chili and carried the bowl to the sink.

“And you said no.” Hope’s tone was sharp, same as when she had cared for her and Chance as young children and they needed discipline. Sera had often thought Hope could have been a teacher, the tone carried such weight.

Sera turned on the hot water and reached under the sink for the dish soap. "I told him I'd get back to him."

The chair scraped as Aunt Hope pushed back her chair. "Last Chance Farm isn't for sale, Serafina. Why, in a few more years, we're eligible for Century Farm designation. I was born and raised in this house. You know our story, our history."

Sera didn't answer. She rinsed the bowl and the spoon and then dried her hands on the towel. Finally she had no other alternative than to face her great-aunt. Turning, she leaned back against the sink. She shook the wrinkles from the towel and folded it in a neat square. "We're out of money, Aunt Hope. I don't have much choice." She didn't have to mention that Aunt Hope had no say in the decision. When her parents had died, her father's share of the farm had been willed to his children as the surviving relatives. Although her brother's name was on the deed, Chance had left home as soon as he graduated high school. She suspected he rarely thought of Last Chance Farm.

"I signed off the deed because I figured it would save fuss when I finally passed. I didn't sign off so you could sell my home out from under me. Does Chance know about this?"

"He does."

If it were possible, the elderly woman actually seemed to shrink before her eyes. Her great-aunt's gaze dropped to the floor, and one wrinkled hand covered her mouth. The hand with the tiny emerald ring. Without a word, she left the room.

Sera walked over to pick up her bowl, still half full. The corn bread, her great-aunt's favorite, had one bite taken out of it. Hope had apparently lost her appetite after Sera's announcement. She covered the bowl with a lid and put it into the refrigerator. Hopefully her great-aunt would finish her lunch later, once she had time to get used to the idea of her home being sold out from under her.

"LET'S GO FIND your mom." Cyrus pushed past Alex and entered the hallway of the spacious home. Alex waited a minute and then shut the door. Lunchtime. Mrs. Kimmel would most likely be found in the kitchen.

Wishing he were already in the city, Alex hung up his coat and picked up Cyrus's from where he had left it on the chair. His father was a stickler for order. The entry had been repainted. Instead of the original off-white, his mother had chosen a pale green, which offset the antiques. The old, mirrored hall tree sat to one side. An entry table held a lamp and a mirror.

He wandered down the hall. His kindergarten picture and high school graduation pictures still hung next to his parents' wedding photo. His memory flashed back to the hallway in the brick house where he had spent the last two nights.

"Alex." Beverly Kimmel threw her arms around her son. "If I didn't know better, I'd say you've grown. You're bigger than I remember."

"Jeez, thanks, Mom. Are you saying I'm fat?" Alex smiled down into his mother's face.

She held his face in her hands. "Hardly. You're skinny as a rail. I just can't believe my son is a grown man. When I think of you—" her eyes glistened for just a minute "—I think of my little boy running around pretending he's a superhero."

"Yeah, well, my superhero days are over."

She laughed and patted his face. "Cyrus, would you go find your uncle? Tell him lunch is ready." She turned to Alex. "I planned a roast beef dinner for last night, but Cyrus tells me the bridge was flooded."

"I'm sorry, Mom. The rain kind of messed up my plans." He didn't say how his weekend plans had gone awry. "Cyrus needed some advice on real estate."

She set the table and filled the stemmed water glasses with iced tea. The glasses had images of flower bouquets on them, which made Alex think of Sera. She would like his mother's glasses.

He sat at the oak table. Last night's roast had been sliced and served cold. She set a small bowl of mayonnaise next to his plate. Leave it to his mother to remember his preferences.

"I'm planning on buying some property nearby so I can increase my herd." Cyrus followed Max Kimmel into the kitchen. Max sat at the end of the oak table, and Cyrus sat across from Alex. "Alex is going to give me an idea of the property's value." Giving his cousin a wink, Cyrus smiled.

Alex caught Max's unsmiling gaze. "Hello, Dad."

Max drank, then set the glass at the point of his butter knife. Only then did he give his son an unsmiling look. "Hello, Alexander. Cyrus didn't give you any choice, did he?"

Alex flushed at his father's astute comment. But then, the man had always been able to see behind people's words. That's what made him such a good attorney and why the townspeople loved him. "Nice to see you, too, Dad."

His mother handed him a knife and a plate with a homemade loaf of bread. He cut two slices and passed it on. "I bought this bread from Sue Hunter. She goes by Sue Campbell now, since she and Brad divorced. She closed The Cookie Jar and just takes orders now. I think a candy store took over her spot. And I hear they put their house up for sale. Too bad. But I have to admit, Suzanna's a lot happier than she used to be. She used to be such a grouch."

"Slow down, Mom." He patted his mother's hand. She was rambling. She did that when she got nervous. Alex searched his brain for a memory of The Cookie Jar and Sue Hunter, but the shop must have opened and closed since the last time he had been home. Although the name Hunter did ring a bell. "The homemade bread smells good."

"She makes cookies, too. I'll send some

with you. You and your dad always liked whoopie pies. I'll bet you don't get good homemade cookies in New York." She handed him a plate of cheese slices and then a jar of pickles.

Alex didn't bother to tell his mother some of the best bakers worked in the city, although he had to admit, there were differences. Whoopie pies in Manhattan were rare.

Alex spread mayonnaise on the bread, added a few slices of cold roast beef and some provolone cheese. The last time he ate a roast beef sandwich was at this very table the weekend after law school graduation. And just before he told his father he had accepted a job in the city. He and his father had barely spoken since. Looking at the distinguished white-haired gentleman to his left, he decided to make an effort. "So how's work, Dad?"

Adding provolone to his own sandwich, his father shrugged. "Just the usual small-town things. Nothing exciting." He took a big bite.

Then Alex remembered where he had heard the name Hunter. The young couple who had picked him and Sera up. "I ran into a Josh Hunter Friday night. He said you helped him out."

His father shrugged again. "You know I can't discuss my cases—" his gaze slid to meet Alex's and just as quickly skittered away "—with strangers outside the office."

"Of course." Alex leaned back in his chair with a sigh. So now he was a stranger. Great. He looked around the kitchen. The refrigerator and stove had been replaced with stainless steel models since he had last been home. His perusal stopped at the entrance to the hall, and he thought of the old house, where penciled lines had marked his growth to manhood. The little house down east had pencil lines in the doorway, too.

His mom smiled brightly. "I've been meaning to ask your mother to meet me for tea, Cy. Have you been to Tea for You?"

In the process of making his sandwich,

Cy shook his head. "I'm more of a coffee drinker. I usually stop at The Wildflower when I'm in town."

"What's The Wildflower?" Alex pictured the cup he had used for coffee while staying at the Callahans'.

"Holly McAndrews's coffee shop. She sells used books, too." Though he had drunk only half his tea, his mother refilled his glass.

"Sera goes to The Wildflower."

His mother set down the pitcher and looked at him. "Sera who?"

Alex wished he had kept quiet. The words had just blurted out. "Callahan."

"Callahan? How do you know her?" His mother's face had the same look she had when he was a kid and she thought he was keeping something from her.

"He spent the night with her." Eyes dancing, Cy took a big bite of his sandwich and grinned at Alex with bulging cheeks.

His mother's eyebrows disappeared underneath her bangs.

"It's not like that, Mom." He gave Cy a look but before he could explain, his father finally spoke.

"That poor girl. Such a tragedy." Max brushed some crumbs from the tablecloth into his hand and then onto his plate.

Cy reached for another slice of bread and proceeded to make another sandwich. "She's a hard worker, that's for sure. Not that she'll be able to keep it up for long. There's just too much work for one person."

"You're making another sandwich?" Alex gave a pointed look to the roast beef hanging from Cy's fingers.

Cy paused, then dropped the meat onto the plate. "Your mother's roast beef is the best. I'm just showing my appreciation."

"We should—"

"You still doing eminent domain cases?"

For a minute Alex didn't realize his father had directed the question to him. He drew his gaze from Cy's plate and met his father's piercing eyes. He had always thought he would not want to come up against his father in court. The man could be relentless. “Eminent domain doesn’t happen that much in my line of work.” Except for the house down east. The one with the pencil lines.

He felt his mother’s hand on his arm. His gaze pivoted to his mother’s soft eyes with the laugh wrinkles at the corners. “Can you stay overnight, Alex? Who knows when you’ll be back?”

He squirmed, uncertain how to explain he had no desire to remain in the tense atmosphere. “I—”

“Two weeks, I hope.” Cy threw the last bite of the second sandwich in his mouth.

This time his gaze rested on the man sitting across from him. “Two weeks? I’m not coming back in two weeks. I did what you asked.”

“Not entirely.”

“I wouldn’t count on Alex if I were you, Cyrus.” Elbows on the table, Max studied the contents of the sandwich inches from his face.

About to take his last bite, Alex threw the crusts onto his plate. "Dad—"

"Pie, anyone?" Beverly stood, smoothing her jeans. "I have coconut cream. Your favorite, Alex. I'll make coffee." She rushed to the counter and threw open the cupboard doors. Quickly finding the coffee, she shut the doors with a bang.

"Thanks, Mom, but we should go." Alex glanced at his cousin, who was busy running a finger over the painted flowers on his iced tea goblet.

"We can't pass up pie, Alex." Cyrus glanced at his watch. "We have lots of time."

Max cleared his throat. "You ever see that old couple you threw out of their home?"

Alex's jaw clenched. "I didn't throw them out of their home. They accepted the company's offer." His father's interpretation of the event that had ultimately and surprisingly appeared on national news made his sandwich taste like cardboard.

"After you threatened them with eminent domain." He cleared his throat, always a precursor to his final argument. "Do you know what happened to them?"

"Why would I? I only oversaw the sale of the property." Despite his loss of appetite, he threw the last bite of sandwich in his mouth. He didn't want to disappoint his mother.

"Sure. Did you know they're living in two separate residences? Married sixty-four years, and you come along and split them up. Unbelievable."

Pushing back his chair, Alex stood. His father was never going to stop. "Thanks, Mom. Lunch was great." He crossed to the counter where his mother stood with a coffeepot filled with water. He put his arms around her. "I love you, Mom." Pulling away from her grip, he left the room.

His mother's voice sounded from the kitchen. "Wait. There's pie. And your cookies."

Grabbing his coat as he passed through

the hallway, he made his escape to the front porch as quickly as possible. His father would never forgive him for not staying in Shadow Falls and joining his firm. How could he know? No one could thrive in the shadow of the great Maximillian Kimmel. He couldn't wait to get back home. Back to New York.

CHAPTER SIX

SHE SAT IN the den, the room at the front of the house where her father's grand piano occupied the space in the corner between two windows. Her mother's big desk occupied the space in the opposite corner. A bookcase behind the desk was filled with gardening manuals and notebooks with her research. Sera sat there and rummaged through the files, looking for the companion planting schedule. Jill Callahan had insisted on using natural pest repellants rather than chemicals.

Even after ten years, Sera still relied on her mother's notes. Bending over the bottom drawer, searching for the file, she couldn't help but think of Cy and his cousin. The lawyer from New York. Somehow she had hoped by not giving Cy a straight answer, she could put the decision off indefinitely, that maybe something would happen to solve their money issues. She shared Hope's wish for receiving Century Farm designation. But she was no better off now than she had been after the accident. She looked up at the sound of a knock. As if her thoughts had summoned him, Cy's burly body filled the narrow doorway from the den into the hall. Rocky stood at his side, like a furry butler announcing a guest.

Clutching his Penn State ball cap, he favored her with a small smile. "Hey, neighbor. Still mad at me?"

She looked down at the pile of papers on her desk. Her mind on the reason for his visit, the words and figures on the lined tablets became a blur. "I thought we were friends, Cy."

"Does that mean I can come in and you won't throw a paperweight at me?"

She glanced at the object on the corner of the desk. "I wouldn't want to break it." She picked up the novelty, a miniature Statue of Liberty. "I bought this on my first trip to New York." She took a breath, remembering the excitement of visiting the big city, when just riding the subway was an adventure. She gestured toward the cushioned chair next to the window. "Sit."

He strode across the wood floor, his boots going silent as he reached the carpet. He settled into the chair with a heavy sigh. "We are friends." Rocky settled at his feet with a grunt.

"I don't appreciate being manipulated."

"I'm sorry." He leaned forward, waiting until she met his gaze to speak. "We talked about this back in January. I've been waiting for an answer. The year's almost half over. I need to make a move as soon as possible. For financial reasons." He leaned back in the chair. Crossing his legs, he grew silent.

Folding her hands together over the mess on the desk, she held his gaze. "So that's why you sneaked your cousin into my home. To do recon."

"As you've already figured out, Alex works for a firm in New York. He'll be back and forth all summer because, like I explained before, the company that's hired his firm is appraising properties in the area for some sort of combination theater and shopping malls. I apologize if you felt I was being duplicitous. I didn't plan on him spending the night here..."

"Serendipity. For you." She picked up a pencil and turned it end to end, tapping the point on the papers. "Aunt Hope doesn't want me to sell."

"Of course not. She's lived here all her life." He leaned forward again, his wind-chapped face serious. "But times change, Sera."

Eraser. Point. Eraser. Point. "She wants us to apply for Century Farm designation."

Cy's gaze dropped to the floor. "I didn't realize your family lived on this property that long."

"My great-grandfather Murdoch won the farm when he picked the winner in a horse race. Almost one hundred years ago. Great-grandmother Moira named the place Last Chance Farm. For obvious reasons. Apparently Gramps had a gambling problem."

"That's quite a story." He lifted his gaze from the floor to hers again. "But it doesn't change the fact you need to make a decision. I hate to be blunt, but you're running this farm into the ground. And the farm is doing the same to you. What kind of friend would I be if I didn't tell you what I see plain as day? You deserve better."

"What am I supposed to do, Cy? I was a year away from earning my degree, but the fact remains I have no degree and few skills. Mom's business is all I have. Not to mention the fact I have two, really three, people to take care of."

"You could go back to school. Somewhere around home this time. I never could understand why you wanted to go all the way to New York City."

"New Jersey, actually. Right across the

river from the city." She dropped the pencil and covered her face with her hands. Planning for the future always left her light-headed and queasy. "I'm just taking things one day at a time."

Cy's voice usually matched his physique, big and booming. But this time, his response was soft. "I'm sorry how things turned out for you. But you've got to think about the future."

She threw her hands up in the air, frustrated with her inability to give Cy a response. "I know."

"Listen, how about if Alex organizes things for you?" Cy's gaze slid from the mess on the desk to the pile of papers on the floor. "I know that legal team from Nashville your father's band sent up here left things in a mess. Alex is good at organization."

Sera followed Cy's gaze from the strewn documents to the disorganized bookshelves and wondered if it were a good idea for the young attorney and her to be in close quarters. The last time she got close to him she had kissed him, like a love-starved spinster. Which, come to think of it, she was.

"HEY, WAKE UP. Do you want to go or not?"

He had been staring at the label of the bottle in his hands, absorbed in the memory. The same drink he had shared with Sera at the airport bar. "What?"

Carrie Oliver sat across from Alex in the dark wooden booth, her hands also wrapped around a bottle. She twirled a curly strand of blond hair around her finger. She always twirled her hair when she was serious about something. "I haven't seen you all week. What does Dad have you working on?"

"The theater shopping complexes." He took a long drink of the hard cider and then wiped the back of his hand across his mouth. "Sorry. I'm worn out from traveling. Do I want to go where?"

She shook her head, her shoulder-length hair just brushing the tops of her shoulders. "I asked if you wanted to go to California in my place next Thursday."

"I'll go." Will Hansen slid into the booth next to Carrie and bumped her with his hip. Friends in first year law school, Will had dropped out to travel and never looked back.

She laughed and elbowed him. "You gave up law school to run a cider bar on the Lower East Side. I'm afraid you don't qualify to interview new associates."

Will shrugged. "I know enough to tell them what they're getting into and to run while they still can." He caught Alex's eye. "Did you and your cousin have a good visit?"

"He was too busy to pick me up. The car rental didn't have any cars left, and I had to catch a ride in a pickup truck held together with baling twine and duct tape." He ran a finger down the condensation on the glass bottle. It reminded him of rain on the windshield, the patter of rain on the leaves and Sera Callahan's impromptu kiss. When his friends remained silent, he realized they were waiting for more of the story, which he had no intention of sharing. "Do you want me to go?"

"I thought maybe you needed a break." She shared a look with Will. "Dad thought you deserved a little break because of the eminent domain fiasco and since, well…"

He lifted the bottle to his lips and let the spicy fermented beverage attack his senses. He returned the bottle to the table with a bang. "Go to California, Carrie. I can handle my end of the deal."

SHE KNELT IN the damp soil and pressed the dirt around the delicate stem of a tomato plant. The sooner the plants were in the ground, the sooner she would have fresh tomatoes for sale at the stand.

Rocky and Lucky lay sprawled in the grass nearby, taking a nap in the warm sun. Overhead a wren warbled. She squinted up at the little brown bird perched at the top of the light pole. "Welcome home, Jenny Wren." She sat back on her heels and straightened her shoulders.

"Think the frost is over?"

Sera started, unaware company stood at the end of the row.

"Good morning, Shawn. I hope so." Smiling, she stood and walked carefully in the area between rows, careful not to tread on the soil around the young plants. "The wren's back."

The hired farmer had lived in the cabin by the apple orchard as long as Sera could remember. She was relieved to see he was up and around, fearful she was asking too much of the older man. Shawn's gaze followed hers to the little birdhouse fastened to the pole just as the brown wren emerged and flew away. "Springtime."

"How are you feeling?"

"Fair to middlin'." Hands stuffed in the pockets of faded jeans, the small man rocked back and forth in scuffed work boots as he studied the results of her last hour's labor. "The sweet corn's looking good."

"You shouldn't have planted that field,

Shawn. The doctor told you to rest. I could've rented the field out."

"Doctor didn't know what he was talking about. All I did was sit on top of the tractor and drive. Besides, the profit margin's greater if we plant. And speaking of cash..."

"I told you I appreciate the offer of a loan, but we're just fine. You hold on to your money. You might need it someday." She felt a twinge of guilt at the thought the man could soon be losing his home, too.

"I consider this farm my home, Sera. If you need help, you ask me. Ya hear?"

"You're as stubborn as Aunt Hope, you know that, Shawn?"

His green eyes twinkled. "I'll take that as a compliment. Looks like you have company, Sera." With a crooked finger to the brim of his faded green cap, he continued on his walk.

Sera watched a large black SUV pull slowly down the drive and park at the trellis. "Who in the world..." She took off her gardening gloves and brushed the dirt from the knees of her jeans. Lucky and Rocky bounced up and ambled in the direction of their company. "Oh, well. What you see is what you get." She walked toward the strange vehicle.

She didn't recognize the visitors until the couple got out of the back seat. Wendy Valentine, black hair as smooth and sleek as ever, waved. "Hi, Sera. I hope you don't mind our just dropping in. We were driving by and I was telling Mom and Dad about your barn."

Only then did Sera recognize the Valentines, the neighbors who had given Aunt Hope a ride home from church.

"Sera, we haven't seen you in a long time." Bernie Valentine strode toward her and clasped her hand warmly. The rotund man with the shock of white hair greeted her as if she were his best friend.

His wife was as small as he was large. Babs Valentine clasped her other hand. "Your great-aunt is such a nice lady. We love spending time with her."

Sera could see where Wendy got her diminutive stature from. She tried to regain her hands, but the Valentines pulled her toward them. Enthusiasm seemed to ooze from their pores.

Wendy, followed by Josh Hunter, approached at a slower pace. "You're probably wondering why we're here." She and Josh looked at each other and smiled that deeply personal smile of young love. Wendy took a deep breath. "We have a request."

Looking at the excited faces of the four, Sera couldn't begin to imagine how she could help the family. "Why don't we go sit on the back porch?"

Wendy held up a hand. Her engagement ring glittered in the morning sun. "Actually, I'd like to walk up to the barn."

"The barn?" Sera still didn't know where the reporter was going with this. Maybe she wanted to do a story on the bank barn. She had asked how old the structure was. "Okay." They walked up the slight incline to the upper story, and

Sera slid open the big barn doors. Pieces of loose hay blew in the sudden breeze entering the cavernous space. “At one time, my grandfather stored loose hay in here. Then, when balers became more common, we stored it in square bales.”

“And now?” Josh ducked as a sparrow flew by on its way outside.

“The barn stays empty. I rent out my fields, and the farmer gives me enough hay to feed my two horses plus a little rent.”

Making themselves at home, Bernie and Babs were already at the far end of the barn examining the square holes in the floor. “How interesting.”

Sera raised her voice so they could hear. “That’s where they used to drop hay down to animals below.”

“So the barn just sits here.” Wendy looked up at the thick hundred-year-old beams. “It’s so beautiful.”

Sera followed her gaze and tried to see the barn as she did. As beautiful. All she saw were bird droppings and moldy hay. "Yep. Just sits here."

Wendy looked at Josh as if for help.

Josh cleared his throat. "We wondered if you wanted to rent out your barn."

Sera leaned forward, sure she hadn't heard Josh. "Do I want to what?"

Josh nervously shifted his gaze from Sera to Wendy and back again. "Would you rent us your barn?"

Sera pulled back. She had heard the man correctly. But what the well-to-do Valentines and the globe-trotting young couple wanted with her barn, she had no clue. "For what? Like a year? I do put the horses in for the winter. Depends what you want to do with it." She didn't bother to mention she wasn't sure she would still own the place come December.

"Just for a weekend." Wendy's brown eyes grew wide as did her smile. Her teeth were perfect. She had a smile that was great for being on television.

"A weekend." Sera surveyed the big barn that had stood for almost a hundred years. The stone foundation was strong, but the white paint on the exterior was fading, and already weeds sprouted around the base. She focused now on the members of the well-dressed group who all seemed to be holding their collective breath while smiling at the same time. "For what, may I ask?"

Josh put his arm around Wendy's waist, prompting, if possible, an even wider smile. "We want a barn wedding."

"A barn wedding." Sera didn't know how to respond. "First of all, congratulations. I'm excited for you." She bit her lower lip. "But aren't there facilities not quite so—" she scuffed her toe through the moldy hay on the floor "—antiquated?"

"We've seen lots of places, but none match this location," said Wendy, her voice full of enthusiasm. "You're right down the road from my parents' house. Josh and I will be on the road all summer. My sister, Katie, is going to handle things."

"With our help, of course." Bernie laid

his big paw on her shoulder. "I've met a lot of people through the years. I could have your barn painted and the interior pressure washed in a jiffy."

At the thought of the expense involved in preparing the barn for a wedding, Sera grew alarmed. "Hold on, Mr. Valentine, I can't afford to hire people."

"I'm not asking you to pay. That would be part of the deal. Plus, a little extra."

Wendy pressed the palms of her hands together and touched her fingertips to her chin. "Please, Sera. A harvest moon wedding. In September. In your barn."

CHAPTER SEVEN

SERA PARKED IN front of Vera Hershberger's small ranch house, and then, with the help of a step stool, assisted Aunt Hope down from the truck and to the front door. Though the day was warm, the woman still carried a sweater in case she got a chill. She had barely said two words to her since Sera's announcement about selling. As was typical with most Callahan disagreements, the subject would only be discussed when matters came to a head. In other words, when Sera signed the papers.

Other than church on Sunday morning, this was the only time Aunt Hope left the house. The women at Vera's always tried to get Sera to quilt with them, lamenting the skill was a fading art, but

Sera took advantage of the opportunity to spend some time relaxing. So, she went to Paris. Pretend Paris.

Meaning, The Wildflower on a Friday afternoon.

Fortunately, she was able to find an empty spot and parked the truck in front of the coffee shop. Across the street someone had planted blue and yellow pansies at the base of the flagpole in the bank parking lot. She walked up the steps and looked up and down the length of the boardwalk. Rocking chairs and potted plants lined the strip. Sue Campbell's no-nonsense black-and-white sign for The Cookie Jar had been painted over with a pastel confection spelling out K&R's Candy Jar.

Pushing open the door of The Wildflower, she heard the now-familiar sounds of French classical music. She glanced at the arrangement of comfy overstuffed chairs at the front window. Empty. Good. She was in no mood for company.

Holly Hoffman McAndrews stood behind the counter, pouring beans into the top of the espresso machine. "Aunt Hope quilting with the church ladies? And you managed to escape?"

The bell over the door dinged as Sera closed it behind her with a laugh. "I'm not a seamstress." She leaned on the counter and waited while Holly finished her task. "Besides, I go to Paris on Friday afternoons right here in Bear Meadows. Have you been to the real Paris?"

Putting the lid on the machine, Holly stepped down and tossed the empty bag away. "Several times when I was based in Germany. We traveled a lot." She rested her chin on her hands and stared into the distance, obviously lost in memories. "Ten years in the air force provided me with a lot of travel opportunities for sure. Now that I'm back home and tied down with a business, the farthest I get to go is Pittsburgh. But I'm cool with that." She smiled.

"Well, your Friday afternoon fake Paris is as close as I'm going to get." She took a deep breath and caught the scent of freshly baked treats. Another reason to enjoy pretend Paris.

"You have Pierre to thank for the tunes. Remember him? He owned the computer store. He gave me his collection of CDs when he left. Told me to play them once a week so we didn't forget him."

"How could we? That French accent of his was so romantic." Sera waggled her eyebrows, then grew serious. "I see The Cookie Jar closed down."

"Sue Hunter, I mean Sue Campbell, is working out of the Reed mansion kitchen. Only taking orders. The candy shop is owned by Kristen and Robin. They're old friends who always talked about starting a small business. You should stop in."

"With my sweet tooth, I'm sure I will." Sera leaned back for a better look at the pastries in the glass case.

The bell dinged, announcing another customer. Sera looked over her shoulder.

A young woman dressed in jeans and a flannel shirt with hair pulled back in a ponytail gave them both a friendly smile as she closed the door. "Hi, Holly."

"Hi, Dr. Hannah." Holly returned her attention to Sera. "Have you met the new vet? She gave Twister and his buddies their shots last week."

Sera shook the vet's hand. "Hi, I'm Sera."

"Do you have horses, Sera?" The woman gave her a friendly smile.

"Two, but my neighbor usually gives them their shots. He picks up the syringes when he buys supplies for his cows."

"You're not talking about Cyrus Carter, are you?" Her eyes brightened as she mentioned his name.

Sera vaguely remembered Cyrus's excuse for not picking up his cousin. He had to meet the new vet. Seeing who the new vet was, she thought, *No wonder.* Dr. Hannah was exactly Cy's type. Athletic and outdoorsy. And with all of his animals, being friends with a vet didn't hurt. "Cy is my neighbor. No offense, but it helps save on the vet bills when he gives the horses their shots."

"None taken. Nice he helps you out."

Holly tapped the counter with her fingers to attract Sera's attention. "I had Sue whip up some croissants yesterday. If you want to pretend you're in Paris, you should have a double espresso and a chocolate croissant. Sound good?"

Sera's mouth watered at the thought of the treat. "I'll be bouncing off the walls, but okay."

Holly winked. "Have a seat and I'll bring it over to you."

"Nice meeting you." Sera smiled at the vet as she walked over to the seating area. She passed by the shelves of used paperbacks and then shuffled through a pile of magazines in the alcove.

She returned to the front window and settled in one of the four brown-and-yellow cushioned chairs clustered around a low table. Two hours to pretend. Resting her head on the back of the chair, she closed her eyes, thinking of the ridiculous request made by the Valentine family. The father had even offered to have the barn repainted as part of the deal. She had, of course, done them a favor and told them no. They couldn't help thinking the barn could be fixed up. They didn't know any better. Wendy and Josh would find another place, more suitable.

She shoved the thought of a wedding in her barn to the back of her mind and let the music transport her. She was at a sidewalk café in Paris, drinking espresso and eating a chocolate croissant. Maybe a handsome Frenchman would stop by and ask her where she was from. A girl could dream, couldn't she?

HE COULDN'T HAVE missed her pickup. When Alex saw the faded blue truck parked in front of The Wildflower, he wheeled the small car into the adjacent parking space, causing the driver behind him to give an angry toot on the horn. "Sorry, buddy."

He wanted to talk to Sera alone, before

Cy tried to run interference. He didn't think it would be this easy. Bad enough he forced himself on unwilling property owners for his work; he wasn't about to do the same thing for a favor for his cousin. Besides, Cy had a way of twisting things to his advantage.

Once again he had flown into Shadow Falls Regional Airport, reserving a rental car himself. Only this time Scooby had overbooked. The kid felt so bad he had loaned him his personal vehicle. So here he was, driving a stick shift compact car with racing stripes. He looked in the cup holder and wondered if Scooby would miss his house key.

Alex walked up the wide steps to the boardwalk and looked up and down the little strip mall. Hair Today to his left. To the right a computer shop, a consignment shop and… His mother was right. K&R's Candy Jar occupied the end storefront, which he assumed had been held by The Cookie Jar. *She likes candy.* He made a detour to the candy shop, returned to the car and then, still looking for Sera, went into the coffee shop.

She sat nestled in a corner, reading a magazine, a demitasse resting on her thigh. When the bell dinged she looked up, down and then back up as recognition dawned. "Alex? What are you doing here?" Setting the cup on the table, she straightened and put her feet on the floor.

"Hi, Sera." He motioned toward the counter. "Let me get a coffee, and then I'll explain. Would you like something?"

She shook her head, but gave him a funny little smile. He could feel her eyes on his back as he walked up to the counter. A tall woman with short, dark hair gave him a welcoming smile. "You look like an amaretto guy."

"Excuse me?"

"I try to guess my customers' preferences. So am I right? Would you like an amaretto?" The woman stood with her hands on her hips and looked him straight in the eye.

"Okay, sure." Alex wasn't used to

bossy baristas. He looked back at Sera, who had returned to reading her magazine. "And—"

"A chocolate croissant. Good choice. Have a seat. I'll bring it all over." She grabbed a cup and turned to the espresso machine before he could answer. He had the feeling he had been dismissed.

He strolled toward the front of the shop and settled into the comfortable chair next to Sera's. "How have you been?" The blue-green eyes gave him a little jolt. *How had he forgotten?*

"Good. You?" She took a deliberate sip from the small cup, as if arming herself for an attack.

"Good." He hesitated before continuing, wondering just how forthright he could be. He leaned forward and touched her knee. "I was hoping I'd find you here."

He would swear she flinched at his touch. "You want to see more of the farm?"

The woman was armed for bear. Well, what did he expect? "No. Well, yes, I guess." Heat suffused his face, and for a minute he felt as if he were sparring with a fellow attorney. "I wanted to see you first."

Holly delivered his drink and croissant, then stood there with her arms folded. She glanced at Sera. "Introduce me to your boyfriend, Sera."

"He is not my boyfriend."

Alex studied Sera's red face, finally deciding she had been insulted by the barista's assumption. He stood to shake the woman's hand. "I'm Alex Kimmel, Cyrus Carter's cousin. From New York."

The woman had a heck of a grip.

"Are you related to Max Kimmel, the attorney?" The barista tilted her head. Her eyes were a slightly more intense green than Sera's.

He grew uncomfortable under her scrutiny. "He's my father." And waited for her response.

"Hmm. Enjoy." Abruptly she walked away.

"How did you get here?"

Lost in his thoughts, he looked up and remembered the reason he had come into the coffee shop. "Flew in, rented a car. Kind of."

Sera laughed. "Scooby had a car for you?"

Her whole face lit up as she teased him. Here, away from her home, she seemed different from the woman he had met at the airport. But, as he settled into the cushioned chair and with the rich scent of roasted coffee in the air, music in the background, he could understand. "Not exactly. He loaned me his private vehicle."

Eyebrows lifted as she took a bite of croissant. "No kidding?"

He nodded. "I guess he felt bad about my last rental fiasco."

Dishes clattered behind the swinging door at the back of the shop. Alex sipped his drink, wondering how exactly to bring up the subject of looking over her deeds.

She saved him the trouble. "Cy came by to see me."

"Good. What did he...have to say?"

"He said you're working in the area on a project for your firm."

He nodded. "I'll be here for a few weeks."

"He suggested you organize my files. But now that I think about it, that's ridiculous. I mean, you're a busy attorney. You don't have time to straighten out my little legal mess." She waved a hand in the air and almost seemed to be talking to herself. "What was he thinking?"

"Actually..." Alex leaned forward and set his cup carefully on the table. "I would be happy to look at your files."

Her eyes narrowed. "You're helping your cousin. In case I sell. I haven't decided, you know?"

He held up both hands. She had gone on the defensive quickly. "I am helping my cousin, I admit. But you should see where you stand anyway. You may not sell to Cy, but you should still have your affairs in order. So what do you say? Do we have a truce?"

She pursed her lips, and he was reminded of the first time he saw her.

Holly came out from the kitchen with a tray of cups just as the front door burst open. The little bell fell to the floor with a clang. "Darn it, Holly, this thing is a pain. You need an electronic buzzer."

"I don't want an electronic buzzer, and the bell only falls off when you or Moose walk in. You two are just so manly the poor bell falls to the floor in terror."

The uniformed man smiled and then walked over to them. "Hi, Sera. How are you and your great-aunt doing?" Dark glasses obscured his eyes, and a badge was pinned to his shirt.

"Hi, Mac. We're fine."

"Do you know whose car is parked next to your truck?" He stood behind the empty chair, hat in hand, and looked from Sera to Alex. He rested one hand on his gun.

Sera tilted her head. Her eyes slipped Alex's way before moving to the magazine in her lap. "What's it look like?"

"White with red racing stripes."

Though her head was bent as she leafed through the magazine, Alex could tell she was biting her lip. He cleared his throat. "Well, I suppose you could say the car is mine."

"Really." The police chief favored him with an appraising look, not unlike the one Alex had received from the barista. He glanced at Sera. "Is he your boyfriend?"

"He is not my boyfriend!" As soon as the words were out of her mouth, Sera covered her mouth with her hand. "Sorry, Mac, that came out louder than I'd intended."

Mac just nodded, his gaze going from one to the other.

Standing, Alex introduced himself. "Alex Kimmel." Again he had the feeling he should be ready for inspection.

The big man shook his hand. "Mac McAndrews, chief of police. Pleased to meet you, Mr. Kimmel."

Alex waited for the inevitable "Are you

Max Kimmel's son?" But he got a surprise.

"Do you know the inspection on your vehicle is expired?" Chief McAndrews crossed his arms. Short sleeves showed muscular and tanned forearms.

"The car inspection? Well, no, how would I know? It's not my car."

"You just said the car was yours. Kind of." A glimmer of a smile. "And the sticker is in the lower left-hand corner of the windshield. Here in Pennsylvania, cars are inspected once a year." The chief took off his sunglasses and looped the earpiece in his shirt pocket. "And your car's inspection has expired."

"Scooby, at the airport, loaned me his personal vehicle." He had a sinking feeling.

"Uh-huh, I'm sorry, Mr. Kimmel, but unless you're taking the car directly to a station, I can't let you drive it."

"You're kidding." Alex sank back down on the cushioned chair, rested his elbows on his knees and stared at the flowered carpet in the seating area. Big, yellow flowers with green leaves. Then he looked at Sera. "Did you have anything to do with this?"

She dropped her feet to the floor and threw the magazine on the table. "Of course not. Ask Scooby." Then she laughed.

"Oh, believe me. I will." He pushed his hand through his hair and glanced up.

The policeman held out his hand. "Could I see your license?"

Alex reached for his wallet and then froze. He looked at Sera. She was biting her lip again. Fighting a smile, he was sure. He kind of liked that.

As soon as the words were out of Mac's mouth, Sera knew for certain Alex's driver's license was still expired. A busy man who didn't drive in the city… Definitely expired. Either way, she knew she was his ride. Unlike the night at the airport, she didn't mind. Maybe Alex wasn't French, but she couldn't deny he was handsome. She pushed the thought to the back of her mind as she left the coffee shop.

"Lucky for you, Mac was in a good mood. You got away with just a warning." Standing at the driver's-side door, she grinned at Alex across the wide expanse of the worn bench seat before hoisting herself behind the wheel.

Using the handgrip, Alex pulled himself into the truck and slammed his door. "If Scooby reports his car stolen, at least the police know where it is."

"We're picking up Aunt Hope. She quilts with the church ladies Friday afternoons." Sera slid him a look. "You'll have to sit in the middle. She can't straddle the clutch."

"I don't mind if you don't mind."

Sera flushed at his teasing tone of voice. "You'll give Aunt Hope someone to talk to. She's not speaking with me at the moment." She turned the key. The engine groaned once, twice, then quit.

"Sounds like Old Blue needs a new battery."

She turned the key again and when the engine started, felt a tiny spark of victory. She backed into the street.

"I can't imagine your great-aunt being angry with anyone, much less you."

"I finally told her Cy offered to buy the farm. Threatening Last Chance Farm gets her dander up a bit." She pulled to the curb in front of the Hershberger home and killed the engine. A retired teacher, Mrs. Hershberger sported a sign that read Go Cubs in her front flower bed.

Alex twisted in his seat and gave her a steady look. "Did you explain?"

She ran a hand over the smooth steering wheel, gathering her thoughts, uncertain how much to share with the cousin of the man who was so desperate to buy her farm. "Callahans aren't the best at talking where feelings are concerned. We prefer to keep our emotions inside until we can't stand it anymore and then blow up all at once."

She shuddered at the memory of some of the family feuds. "More exciting that way."

His slow smile warmed her from the inside out. "My family prefers a low simmer." He took her hand from the steering wheel. "After I turned down his offer of a job, my father has barely said two words to me in the last six years."

She wanted to ask him more, but over his shoulder she saw her great-aunt coming out the front door. Rose Hoffman had her arm through the crook of her friend's elbow. Together they came down the front steps and along the short walkway.

Sera withdrew her hand from his grip. "Stay here." When she came around the truck with the little step stool, her great-aunt was smiling. For a minute Sera hoped the disagreement was forgotten, but when she reached for Hope's arm, the older woman brushed her away and instead took Alex's hand. They were chatting away by the time Sera climbed behind the wheel.

"Vera was telling me how much your

father helped with the issue between Hank Hershberger and Josh Hunter."

Sera's gaze strayed toward Alex, curious how he would respond. If he and his father had hardly spoken, he probably wasn't crazy about the idea of discussing his family issues. "Yes, ma'am."

"Your father has helped a lot of people in town with legal problems. Why don't you work with your father?"

He probably didn't realize he was doing it, but Sera noticed a muscle in his jaw twitch before he answered her great-aunt. "I did my internship in the city with the father of a classmate. I planned to come back home, but I figured I should get some experience. Then—" he hesitated "—one thing led to another and I was offered a job."

Sera had the feeling Alex's family had had a few feuds of their own. Maybe he did understand.

"Your father is such a good man."

"I almost forgot." Alex reached into his

pocket and withdrew two boxes. "Candy from the new candy shop."

"Well, aren't you the thoughtful one?" Aunt Hope beamed as she accepted a box.

"This one's for you, of course." Tapping a finger on the lid, Alex held on to the second box. Throwing him a thank-you smile, Sera turned into the lane, thinking how deftly Alex had changed the subject with his surprise. The man obviously didn't want to talk about his father. Absently she noted the fence could use a coat of paint. Yet another reason not to have a crowd descend on the farm for a wedding. She pulled the truck close to the back gate. "After I help Aunt Hope into the house, I'll take you to your cousin's."

"Why don't you stay for supper, Alex?" Hope patted his arm. "Jean doesn't always cook on Fridays."

Sera caught Alex's uncertain look. "Sure, why not?" At least with Alex, she was assured of a friendly face at the supper table. And what harm did having him around do? As much as Aunt Hope might regret signing over the deed, Sera would make the final decision. Chance certainly didn't care. And the guy was getting good at providing her with chocolate just when she needed it.

CHAPTER EIGHT

HE FOLLOWED HER down the dark hall and into the front room. "You play piano?" Dinner had been homemade vegetable soup and bologna sandwiches.

"No." Sera ran a hand over the top of the instrument and stopped at a photograph, which she handed to him. The picture showed a smiling man with a thick head of dark hair at a piano surrounded by musicians. "My dad was in an Irish band that toured the country. County fairs, convention centers, you name it. California to Maine. Anyplace to make a buck. He could play anything. My brother takes after him."

He replaced the photograph on the lace doily. The frame next to it contained a wedding picture. "Your parents?"

She nodded.

He picked it up and studied the woman's features. "You have your mom's smile."

She leaned over his shoulder. "You think so?"

Her hair tickled his cheek. Clearing his throat, he set the frame back in the right spot. "Definitely."

Resting her gaze on the two photographs, her smile was wistful. "They were an interesting couple. Dad was on the road a lot, and Mom was content to keep the home fires burning." She tilted her head and she gave him a serious look. "At least I think she was. But they seemed to complement each other."

She led the way to the rolltop desk in the corner. Following her, Alex stopped at a framed photograph on the wall next to the fireplace. "This is interesting."

She looked up. "Apple orchard in bloom." She joined him and studied the picture. "I took that picture around this time of year. I like how the light shines through the petals. There's a pinkness about the shot. You see what I mean?" She pointed to a corner of the picture.

"I do. You're talented."

"I used to be." She returned to the desk, where the stacks of paper had been since his last visit. She picked a manual off the floor and returned it to the bookcase, itself a disorganized mess of notebooks, novels and reference books.

"How did your parents die, Sera?" If he hadn't been studying her so intently, he would've missed the slight stiffening of her shoulders. With a final shove, the manual disappeared and she turned. "Plane crash."

"I'm sorry." She didn't want to talk about her parents either, although for different reasons than his. He had a feeling she didn't want to turn around until she was in control of her emotions. "That's why you were in the bar. You were waiting for Al to tell you the plane to Detroit made it out."

She shrugged. "You never know." Propping her hands on her knees, she bent over the pile of papers on the floor. "I should've cleaned this up long ago, but I just never seem to be able to catch up. Maintenance records, invoices for repairs, renewal notices. If you can make some sense of it, well, that would be appreciated. So, I guess we have a truce."

He leaned in close. "You've taken on quite a lot of responsibility."

Her chest rose as she took a deep breath and seemed to shrink back against the bookcase. "Somebody had to. My brother was only eleven at the time." She pushed past him and headed for the hallway. "I have things to do. Don't forget to call your cousin."

He stood in the den and watched her flee into the hallway and up the stairs, and wondered what would happen to Hope and Sera when Cy bought the farm.

Wanting to call Carrie as well as his cousin, he walked up to the orchard to get a signal. When he reached the top, he stopped in amazement. In the two weeks he had been gone, the apple trees had blossomed into a riot of pink and white. It looked just like the photograph in the study. Though early evening, a few bees still buzzed around the petals. He found a rock at the edge of the orchard overlooking the stream far below.

"My favorite cousin, where are you?" His cousin's booming voice prompted him to put the phone on speaker and hold it away from his ear.

"I'm in the orchard and can see your silos. You have an American flag flying from the big one. Very patriotic."

"Sera's orchard? When did you get in? And I'm a patriot, by the way."

"Noon." Alex swatted at a curious bee buzzing near his shirtsleeve.

"You flew in? Did you rent a car? I would've come to get you."

"My luck at renting cars has run out." He told his cousin about Scooby's car. His cousin's deep laugh prevented him from finishing his story.

"Oh, man. Leave it to you. Why don't you just buy a darn car? You're making enough money working for that fancy law firm."

"I don't need a car in the city. Flying saves time."

"Obviously not."

Through a ceiling of pink petals, Alex saw a hint of blue sky. Sera was right. The air did look pink.

"So how did you run into Sera?"

"I saw her truck at the coffee shop. I wanted to make sure she was okay with me going forward."

"You didn't think I handled it?" His voice grew deeper.

"You've been a bit remiss so far."

"We talked. She's agreed to let you look through the deeds she has at the house. That will give you a head start on the title search. Make sure everything's good to go."

"She's wavering. She's not sure she should sell."

"Don't forget whose side you're on, cousin."

"Who said anything about sides?

Shouldn't she do what's best for her family?"

When there was no response, Alex checked his phone to see if the call was dropped. The line was still open. "Cy?"

"What about what's best for *your* family, Alex?"

Maybe he didn't realize he was taking sides. He should remain impartial. "You're right. Listen, why don't you come pick me up?"

"I'll be over as soon as I can."

"See you soon." Alex ended the call and stared across the creek. In the distance the long line of ridges stretching on either side of the wide valley were just beginning to turn green.

He called Carrie, who was still in California. "How'd the interview go? Do we have a new colleague?"

"Maybe. I'm going to stick around for the weekend and play tourist. Fly back Monday. Do you mind?"

"Why should I mind?"

"We should be more involved in each other's cases."

"Why? In case I get hit by a truck?" Alex shook his head, puzzled at his colleague's comment.

"Either of us could get hit by a truck… or something."

"I'll be sure to look both ways when I cross the street."

"We'll talk about this when I get back. Take care, Alex."

He leaned back against the tree and wondered if Carrie thought he wanted to leave the firm, to return home. And even if he did, the formerly open door to his father's office was firmly shut. Surely she wasn't thinking of leaving? The sun warmed his skin and he shut his eyes, grateful for once to be out of the city, to have no one making demands on his time. The bees droned as they flitted among the pink petals. At least it wasn't as quiet as the day he and Sera had sat here in the fog. His chin dropped to his chest. He struggled to keep his eyes open, but failed as sleep overcame him.

"You want to buy our home?" The top of the old woman's head barely comes up to his chin, but her grip is firm. She peers up with bright blue-green eyes. "Where will we go?" She settles into a rocking chair and begins to knit, her needles going faster and faster, the clicking like angry bees.

Alex looks up, recognizes the glass door. Why is the old woman sitting in front of his office building in the financial district? Suit-clad men and women hustle by, briefcases in hand. "What are you doing here?"

"We have nowhere to go." Bending over, she pulls an old-fashioned percolator from alongside the building and then a brown cup from a cloth bag. Yellow script spells out The Wildflower. *"Cup of coffee?"*

"This is your last chance, son."

Alex whirls around. His parents sit in matching recliners on the other side of the big glass doors. "Dad? Mom? What are you doing here?"

His father leans forward, a glint in his eye. "Remember, son. This is your last chance."

"Cup of coffee?" A hand gripped his shoulder and was giving it a shake. Alex woke.

"Looks like you could use a cup of coffee, son." He wasn't a big man, but the smile in the round face was wide. His green cap matched his eyes.

He sat up. The sun was just touching the tops of the ridgeline in the distance, turning the sky above into a ribbon of orange and pink. How long had he slept? And what did his father mean? *This is your last chance, son.* Last chance for what? And who was this guy with the green cap?

"So how about that cup of coffee? I live just down over the hill." The man lifted a walking stick and pointed toward the log cabin with the stone chimney.

"No. No, thank you."

"Suit yourself." With a finger to his green cap and heading in the direction he had pointed, the man soon disappeared among the trees in the lower orchard, leaving Alex to wonder if he were still dreaming.

Alex walked down the dirt road thinking about pink petals, the familiar green eyes and the man with the green cap who had offered him a cup of coffee. He spotted Cy kneeling in the gravel next to a faded red truck with a dent in the front fender. "Where's your new truck?"

Cy scratched Rocky behind the ear. The dog moaned in appreciation. "I don't use the new truck when I'm working."

Alex glanced toward the kitchen door. "Have you seen Sera?"

Cy shook his head. "Nobody around."

Alex was reluctant to leave without saying goodbye, but considering how she had run off, he suspected she wanted to be alone. "Let's go, then."

Driving back to Clover Hill Farms with his cousin, Alex looked Cy up and down.

"Don't you think you should clean up a little before you come over to Sera's? And you're missing a button on your shirt."

"Why?" Cy brushed a hand over the ground-in dirt on the knees of his jeans. "I'm not asking her to marry me."

Alex grabbed a handgrip over the window as Cy bounced across a rut in the road. "Maybe you should. It would be a heck of a lot easier than going through that pile of papers in the den. I'm guessing her parents didn't leave a will."

"Jack never got around to it. His band sent up their own attorneys from Nashville. I don't know the whole story, but I heard Jack had borrowed on his share of the tour for some project he was doing."

"What was it?"

"No clue. But, yeah, I'm not surprised the papers are a mess." He drummed his fingers on the steering wheel. "You really think I should marry her?"

Wishing he hadn't mentioned the thought, Alex clenched his jaw. "How should I know? But the girl sure has a mess on her hands."

Cy parked next to the back porch and led the way into the kitchen. Even before he mounted the porch steps Alex could smell the enticing scent of freshly baked pie.

His aunt was just taking the pie out of the oven when they entered. "Did you have supper, Alex?"

"Hi, Aunt Jean, I did."

Cy disappeared down the hall.

Alex walked over and inspected the pie. Slits in the crisp brown sugary crust oozed purple. "What kind?"

"Raspberry. We usually just have dessert Friday nights."

He caught her eye. "Have any ice cream?"

"As a matter of fact, I do." She pushed him toward the kitchen table. "Have a seat."

"Where's Uncle Bob?" Alex sat at the gray Formica table he remembered from breakfasts shared with his cousin the few times he had stayed overnight. Some things never changed.

"In the basement. I thought the smell of this pie would bring him upstairs, but I must have been wrong. I'm glad you're here. Otherwise I'd never have any company. Cy is always working, and Bob is down in the basement fixing up that boat." She withdrew three bowls from the cupboard and set them next to the pie, cooling on top of the stove.

"Aunt Jean, I was up in Sera's orchard and I ran into some little guy with a green cap."

She laughed as she bustled around the kitchen. "You met Shawn."

Just watching his aunt dart back and forth made Alex tired. "Who's Shawn?"

She finally stopped and leaned against the counter, a red dish towel in her hands. "Their hired man. I don't think he does much of anything now. He's getting up there in years." She turned and glanced at the pie, as if debating whether she wanted to cut it or not.

"So Sera does have help."

Her eyes still on the pie, she answered without looking at him. "I heard he was down with pneumonia this spring."

"He roused himself to plant her sweet corn. I was hoping to rent those fields." Cy entered the room wiping his face and hands with a towel. "Where's my pie?"

Jean swatted him with the dish towel. "Just be patient. I'm letting it cool." She waved her hand over the pie. "Shawn was a Vietnam vet wandering the country back in the sixties. He was from down South somewhere but apparently had no family left. Sera's grandfather, the original Chance Callahan, took a liking to him and offered him a job. He's been here ever since." She touched her fingers to the pie. Apparently satisfied, she pulled a butter knife from the drawer and sliced the pie in two.

Cy searched the freezer and pulled out a container of ice cream. "He's not much help to Sera anymore. He should be retired, like Dad. The sooner Sera accepts that the better."

Jean handed Alex a bowl with a still-steaming piece of pie and a large helping of ice cream. He waited while Jean and Cy got their own and Cy returned the ice cream to the freezer. "You always did make the best pies, Aunt Jean."

"Thank you, Alex." She settled into her chair with a satisfied smile. "At least you appreciate my efforts."

Behind his mother's back, Cy mimed punching him. He sat and patted his mother's hand. "I tell everyone you're the best cook in the world, Mom." He dug into his dessert with a happy grin.

"Do you think Sera will sell?" Alex directed his question to his aunt. She knew the family better than anyone.

"The Callahans can be a stubborn bunch. But she always liked Cy."

"Not that much." Cy made a face.

"You went to the prom together."

Cy sat back in his chair and shot Jean

a look. "Thanks to you and her mother. We had nothing to do with it."

"Still, I thought maybe someday you and she would get together." She slanted a glance at her son. "Give me some grandchildren to spoil."

Despite the mouthful of ice cream and pie, Cy managed to frown. "Don't get your hopes up, Mom."

"She works so hard. You should do something nice for her."

"I gave her a truckload of firewood. Wasn't that nice?"

"Nice maybe, but not romantic. Sometimes I think she needs to be reminded of what she's been missing stuck on that farm."

After listening to the discussion, Alex thought of the Statue of Liberty paperweight he had seen on her desk. "You should take her to New York."

"City?" Cyrus threw him a look of irritation. "She went to school right across the river. What makes you think she'd want to go back?"

"Because it's been ten years. That's a wonderful idea, Alex. New York in springtime. Maybe there's still hope for grandchildren." Jean's eyes lit with glee.

"Take her to the city. Show her a good time. If you're really thinking about—" he had a hard time saying the word "—marrying her, you need to change your approach." He glanced at Cy's faded jeans and plaid shirt with the missing button. "Big-time."

They were just finishing their pie and ice cream when the door to the basement opened with a bang. His flannel shirt covered with sawdust, Uncle Bob stood at the top of the cellar steps. He stared at their empty bowls with sad hound-dog eyes. "Where's mine?" He looked puzzled at the laughter following his words.

CHAPTER NINE

CY'S INVITATION TOOK her by surprise. The closest they had ever come to a date was the senior prom. Since neither of them was dating anyone at the time, their mothers came up with the idea to send them together. So they did. Though they stayed out the entire evening, they were surrounded with friends. She hadn't even kissed him good-night at the door.

So when he offered her a June weekend in New York she was speechless. When she had protested, saying she couldn't leave Aunt Hope alone, Jean Carter intervened and invited Hope over for the weekend.

Cy suggested they both fly to the city in his little Cessna. She knew he was busy with spring planting and cows having calves so he was trying to save travel time. But the thought of being thousands of feet in the air with nothing between her and the ground but a sheet of aluminum paralyzed her with fear. She considered refusing the offer, but the temptation to see the city again was too great. She offered to take the bus, insisting Cy fly up and meet her.

So here she was, on the upper deck of a double-decker bus motoring down Interstate 80 to New York City. Three hours into the trip, the bus stopped at a convenience store. Her stomach growled. With the early pickup in Shadow Falls, she had barely made it to the bus stop on time much less have breakfast. She grabbed a chili dog and chips and returned to her seat on the bus.

When she saw the Statue of Liberty in the distance, her heart rose into her throat. The years dropped away and she was eighteen again, just out of high school, arriving at Clark University in Hoboken on a scholarship. Her parents had been so proud. She had loved the city with the occasional trips home. Then the accident, and suddenly she was guardian to an eleven-year-old and caretaker to a woman in her eighties.

She inspected her nails. Clean, but short. She dug out a bottle of nail polish. As she painted her nails, the fumes actually made her gag. The weaving of the bus also didn't help. By the time the bus pulled into the terminal, she was nauseous. She looked around, expecting to see Cyrus towering above everyone. Despite having to take a taxi from the airport, he still would have arrived sooner than she.

Exiting the bus terminal, she found a bench and checked her phone. Nothing. She looked up and down the side street facing the entrance to the terminal. Bright orange cones narrowed the two-way street to one way, causing the traffic to back up. The heat and humidity seemed to hold the exhaust fumes close to the ground. She leaned her head against the brick wall and shut her eyes. She never should have come. The garden needed watering and weeding. Feeding the animals was too much to ask of Shawn, still weak from his bout with pneumonia.

"Sera."

She opened her eyes. Ten feet away, a couple waved down a taxi. Maybe she should get a taxi. Then she realized Cy hadn't mentioned the name of the hotel.

"Sera." She did hear her name. To her left a box truck unloaded mattresses for the store across the street. She looked to her right. Pushing through a trio of laughing women, a man in a gray suit lifted his arm and waved, but a woman exiting the terminal waved back.

She checked her phone again.

"Sera." She noticed the man in the gray suit was standing directly in front of her.

Her gaze traveled up the neatly pressed pants to the apricot tie and matching pocket handkerchief to brown eyes. Her stomach flipped. "Alex?"

Looking left and then right as people pushed past, Alex joined her on the bench. “How was your trip?”

As her stomach continued to churn, Sera didn’t see the point in engaging in niceties. She didn’t spend six hours on a bus to see this man. “What are you doing here?”

Avoiding her gaze, Alex eyed the men unloading the mattresses. “My cousin called in a favor.”

Studying his face, Sera concluded Alex wasn’t much happier than she was. “Your cousin asks a lot of favors from you.” She should have gone with her gut. Not the one that was presently giving her tiny shots of pain, but the one that had warned her she would be better off staying home and working. Because instead of enjoying a weekend in the city with her old friend Cy, she was stuck in the city with Cy’s cousin, the annoying but definitely well-dressed attorney.

SHE PULLED HER hand away when Alex reached for it. “The streets are packed, Sera. We can’t get separated.”

He had been sitting at his desk, working on one of the theater shopping mall projects, but he had been thinking about Sera. About Cy picking her up, showing her the city, how her blue-green eyes would light up with pleasure. When his phone signaled a text, he stared at the message on his phone. As his father was fond of saying…unbelievable. Cyrus wasn't coming. Then he remembered the trip, which Jean had pounced on, had been his idea. Cyrus hadn't been crazy about the idea from the start. For a big man, Cy was a big chicken. Texting instead of calling. *Who does that?*

"So why are you here instead of Cy?" She kept her hands pressed to her stomach, as if she were afraid to touch him.

"Three of his prize cows are having calving difficulties. Cy had to call the vet. He said he'll fly up in the morning." He reached for the small overnight bag by her feet and then stood up.

"The vet, huh? Figures." She remained

seated, her hands still at her stomach. "Maybe I should go back home."

"Nonsense. I have… I mean, Cy has the weekend planned." He looked around, anxious to get away from the crowded bus terminal. "I suppose we should check into the hotel first and get rid of your suitcase."

She lifted her gaze. "I didn't make a reservation. Cy was supposed to do that."

"I've taken care of it." He reached again for her hand. This time she took it.

SHE OPENED HER eyes and instantly her brain began to puzzle over the events of the previous evening. She had been sick. Extremely sick. She remembered pressing her sweating forehead against the cool tiles of the bathroom floor, changing into shorts and a T-shirt. Someone had wiped her face with a damp cloth and helped her back to bed. She wasn't home because her sheets were white, not dark brown. Where was she? The hotel. She closed her eyes and just appreciated the feel of the cool, crisp sheet against her cheek. Cy had picked a nice hotel where people took care of sick customers. She smiled. In the distance she heard an announcer's voice giving a play-by-play of a baseball game. The New York Yankees. Of course.

A male voice asked, "Feel like a cup of tea?"

Her eyes popped open. The maid? Were maids male? Her gaze focused on the nightstand next to the bed. A wallet and a handful of change.

"I can make you some toast if you're up to it."

She rolled over and squinted at the backlit form filling the doorway. She rubbed her eyes and looked again, certain she must be dreaming. "Alex?" She struggled to sit.

Alex set a cup on the nightstand and gently pushed her back against the pillow. "You should take it easy. You were pretty sick last night."

"What happened?"

He sat at the foot of the double bed, pushed into a corner of the small room. "I think the chili dog turned on you."

She groaned. At the same time she realized what she must look like. She tried to smooth her hair, but her fingers kept getting tangled in the knots. "Where am I?"

"My place." He handed her the cup. "I had booked you in to a hotel in Times Square, but I didn't think you should be alone last night. This was easier and closer."

The tea slid down her throat. The warmth spread through her belly. "You're being awfully nice to me."

"Despite your opinion, I'm not a bad guy."

She handed him the cup and then lay back against the pillow and studied him. "Did you wipe my face with a washcloth?"

"My mom used to do that for me." Making himself more comfortable, he stretched one leg along the foot of the bed. The gray suit pants had been replaced by gray sweatpants. "I remember it always helped."

The heat moved up her neck and onto her cheeks at memories of the previous night. She covered her face with her hands. "You watched me throw up."

"No big deal."

She peeked through her fingers. He was smiling. "I must look a fright."

"You look pretty good, considering. You're lucky you didn't eat much yesterday."

"Cy. When does Cy get here?" She sat up and then grimaced as pain shot through her belly. She pressed a hand to her stomach and leaned back against the headboard.

He glanced out the room's single window, which looked out onto a fire escape and the neighboring brick building. "It's raining."

She followed his gaze. The curtainless window was streaked with rain. "I see, but when does Cy arrive?"

Alex seemed to be looking everywhere

but at her. "He can't fly in bad weather. He's only VFR rated. Visual flight rules, you know? When I told him you were sick..."

She glanced down into her cup, absorbing the news, knowing she should be disappointed. And yet she wasn't. "Knowing Cy, he probably said good thing he didn't fly all the way up here for nothing." Alex's embarrassed glance at the floor told her she was close to the truth.

"He did plan on taking you around the city. Rockefeller Center, Empire State Building. We can still do that if you're up to it."

The thought of traipsing through the city under cloudy skies caused her to rub her belly. "I don't think I'm ready. But don't let me keep you from anything."

"It's a rainy Saturday. I'd be at home whether you were here or not."

"Besides, I've already seen the sights." She ran a hand over the chocolate-brown sheet. Soft. High thread count.

"Cy mentioned you went to school not far from here." Alex sounded skeptical, as if he could hardly believe the country girl had been educated in the city.

She realized that Alex's impression of her was of a young woman afraid to leave home. "It was a long time ago, but we used to come into the city quite often."

"What was your major?"

She smiled at the memories. At his look of interest she continued. "I received a scholarship to Clark Institute of Technology. Majored in science communication and minored in music and technology."

Alex's mouth dropped open. His only response was "Wow."

"Who would've guessed, right?" Sera felt a sense of accomplishment at rendering the man temporarily speechless. "Little ole me in the big city."

"But you didn't finish."

Somehow the forced intimacy of the rain outside, sitting together on the bed, made telling the story a little less difficult. "Ten years ago our family was in great shape. Dad was on the road. His band was booked solid nine months out of the year. Mom had a successful produce business. I was in my third year on a full scholarship." She sipped her tea, which had gone cold. She set the cup on the nightstand and glanced up at Alex, who remained quiet. "You don't want to hear this, do you?"

"I'm curious why you didn't finish, but if the telling of the story is too much..."

She shrugged. "The story is years in the past. I should be able to talk about it by now, don't you think?"

Alex slid sideways, propping himself on the mattress with one elbow. "Some people never get over things no matter how far in the past they are."

"But I want to. I want to move on." She felt a sudden resolve and sat up straighter, as if doing so would help the story emerge from her memories. "Dad had been home for a month, busy completing Mom's list of chores. He was supposed to fly into Buffalo to meet the rest of the band at the beginning of March. Mom wasn't preoccupied with what was growing in the fields yet, so he asked her to go along. They wanted to run up to Niagara Falls for a little side trip." She paused, pursing her lips, remembering the phone call from Aunt Hope. "The plane went down. A late winter storm caused icing. I came home. Chance was devastated. I never went back."

Alex scooted up next to her and pulled her into his arms. Sera squeezed her eyes shut to hold back the tears. Ten years. Her voice was a whisper. "Why cry after ten years?"

Alex didn't say a word. He just patted her back and held her tight.

HE GOT THE idea when she fell asleep in his arms. Cy was determined to buy her farm which, obvious to anyone, was steadily going downhill. The young woman had set goals before, she could do so again.

He eased her onto the pillow and inched

down to the bottom of the bed. Trying to work quietly in the next room, he studied the theater mall account and then made some phone calls. By late afternoon he heard her stirring. He was watching a second game when she appeared in the door. "You have some color in your face."

"I feel much better." She padded over to the living room window. In the distance the setting sun lit the underside of the storm clouds. She looked down. "What a pretty street. Where are we?"

"The Lower East Side."

"I thought you would live on the Upper West."

"I moved here for an internship and got to like the neighborhood. There's a guy two doors down who makes the best homemade soups. Archie moved here from Greece. If you're hungry, I'll go get some."

She settled on the opposite end of his couch and wrapped her arms around her bare legs. "Maybe in a little bit. I'm still a little groggy."

"More tea?"

"No, thank you. You've been an excellent host."

"You're surprised, aren't you?"

"Maybe a little." She looked around the apartment. "I should check to see if there's a bus leaving anytime soon. I've outstayed my welcome, I'm sure." She gave him a sideways look.

"No, you haven't. I'm enjoying your company." His reply seemed to throw her off balance. "You might as well stay and go back tomorrow as planned."

"I suppose I could." She was quiet for a minute. "Where do your parents stay when they visit?"

He smiled inwardly at her change of subject. "Dad doesn't visit. When Mom comes up for a show and to shop, I give her the bed and I take the couch."

"The good son." She propped her chin on her knees. "You don't talk about your dad much. You don't get along?"

"He didn't take kindly to my accepting a job here in the city." At the sound of wild applause from the television, he returned his gaze to the screen.

"Do you think you'll ever move back home?"

"I'll never say never, but Dad's found a new reason to criticize me. He's not too happy with a decision our company made recently."

"Which was?"

He watched a player round third base and wished the subject would go away. Like a bad penny, the topic kept turning up. "We used the eminent domain law to force an elderly couple to sell their home. They had no children and were forced to move into a nursing home. Well, turns out the nursing home in their area couldn't accommodate the husband because he was diagnosed with dementia." He looked up. "So they were separated."

"Oh, boy. I don't know your dad, but from what I've heard about him he wouldn't stand for that outcome."

Her response took him by surprise. She was absolutely right. His father would have insisted on a different outcome. Alex had just pushed the whole affair to the back of his mind. "The last time I was home, my father asked me if I was there to throw him and Mom out of the house."

"Nice." She kept her chin on her knees and stared into space. "Have you checked other facilities in their area?"

"Their property was in eastern Pennsylvania. I assumed somebody had."

"Maybe not. Maybe there are facilities that could keep them together as a couple."

"We've moved on from that job. It's in the construction phase now."

"It's not your job, I know, but there's nothing stopping you from doing a little research, is there? Going back to see them?"

Alex thought for a minute. "No, I suppose not."

"You might feel better about the whole issue if you can offer a solution." She stood and stretched. "Since I'm staying, why don't I shower, and then we'll check out that soup?"

Alex watched her walk back into the bedroom and shut the door. All this time he had been thinking she was the one who needed help. Her simple comment made him realize…he could accept a little advice, as well.

"ARE YOU SURE you're up for this?" Alex inspected Sera's face for signs of strain, but she looked happy to be outside in the morning sun. The rain of the day before had blown out to sea. Church bells rang in the distance.

"I'm starved. Archie's soup last night was great, but my belly is still empty." She lifted her face to the sun and breathed deep. "Wow, what's this heavenly aroma?"

Alex pointed to a storefront. The smell of fresh bread wafting along the quiet street was an everyday occurrence. Sera reminded him the aroma of baking was one of the great things about the small neighborhood. "Another reason not to move."

"Is this your favorite bagel place?" Sera

reached for his hand and they crossed the narrow street.

Minutes later they were sitting at the counter that stretched along the length of the front window. "Are you up for walking? I had an idea yesterday."

"I'm fine. Believe me. The chili dog is long gone." She smiled and spread cream cheese on a plain bagel. "What are you having?"

"A whole wheat everything with sun-dried-tomato cream cheese." He took a bite and closed his eyes in ecstasy. When they finished they stood outside the shop, then he led her toward the center of town. "Tell me about your parents."

"My dad, Jack, was the life of the party. It's funny, now that I think about it, the farm came down through his family, yet he was rarely home. His grandfather won the farm after betting on a horse race."

"You're kidding. The whole farm?"

Sera nodded. "And Great-grandmother Moira told him if he gambled again, she was gone. The farm was his last chance."

"Sounds like a tough woman." He elbowed her in the side. "Like someone else I know." The look she threw his way warmed his heart. Shy and proud at the same time.

"Aunt Hope was born the year after Murdoch and Moira moved to the farm. My grandfather didn't come along for another ten years, like Chance and I. In fact, my brother was named after him." She slanted a look his way. "That's why the decision to sell has been so difficult. Aunt Hope has her mind set on Last Chance Farm receiving Century Farm designation."

The smile had faded. Alex tried to think of a way to bring it back. "Tell me about your mom."

"That's just it. Last Chance Farm came down through the Callahan family, but my mom, Jill, was the one who stayed and managed the place. She was the stable influence in our family while my dad jumped around the country having fun. Why, his band even went to Ireland once."

They came out on Fifth Avenue. Alex took her elbow and steered her north. "Wait a minute."

She looked up with a smile. "What?"

"Did you just say your parents' names were Jack and Jill?"

Sera laughed. "Can you believe it? But they were quite the team. Mom keeping the home fires burning, allowing Dad to chase his dreams. But they both seemed content, and in the end, isn't that what matters?"

They had walked quite a distance as Sera related her family history. When Alex stopped, she stared at the structure before them. Alex waited for her reaction, hoping after all this time she would be happy with the arrangements he'd made.

"The library." She gave him a quizzical look.

"They've done some renovations since you've been here for a visit. I thought you'd like to see."

"Definitely. I love this place." Her face

lit. "I hear they restored the Rose Reading Room. Can we go inside?"

He breathed a sigh of relief. Maybe his surprise would work out after all. They passed the two stone lions guarding the entrance and took the elevator to the third floor. Walking through the Rose Reading Room, they admired the restored beauty of the ornate ceiling and the murals, not rushing to move on. Eventually, they went back down to the main hall.

Sera started for the doorway, then stopped and gave him a look. "You keep checking your watch. Do you have an appointment?"

"I do."

"I can find something to do. I could wander around here all day. Did you see the little train carrying books from one floor to another?"

Growing more excited, he pulled her across the entry. "Actually, you have an appointment."

"Me?" Her brow wrinkled.

A woman rose as Alex brought Sera to

a table in a side room and then gave him a hug. "Alex. It's nice to see you again."

"Nomi, this is the woman I told you about. Sera Callahan. She's from Bear Meadows, Pennsylvania." He turned. "Sera, this is Nomi Harper. She works in Admissions at Clark."

He left the two women. Sera still looked puzzled. Nomi was busy clicking away on her laptop. His decision the day before, as Sera slept in his bed, to call an old friend working at Clark, had paid off. The question was whether Sera would take advantage of the opportunity. Waiting out front next to one of the lions, he watched the multitude of people, cars, buses and taxicabs going up and down the street.

When Sera finally appeared, the look on her face could only be described as pensive. "What are you doing?"

He motioned over his shoulder at the stone lion. "I'm keeping Patience company. Or maybe this one is Fortitude. He looked lonely."

Sera settled in next to him. "You know what I mean. Why did you set up that meeting?"

He looked up at the massive structure of the New York Public Library. He had guessed correctly that Sera would want to see something meaningful, something that was once part of her educational experience. What he didn't know was if she was ready to make a change. He hoped for the best and took the plunge. "If Cy buys your farm, you need to make plans for yourself. You said your dream was to finish college. I met Nomi years ago when we both volunteered on an art project in Bryant Park. I knew she could answer any questions you'd have about returning to school after an absence."

Sera just stared at the stream of adults and children hurrying in and out of the building. "She was a wealth of information. She offered to see if my scholarship could be reinstated." She inspected her nails, a pretty shade of pink. "But, Alex, I haven't yet decided to sell. There's Aunt

Hope and Shawn and Chance to think about. This decision doesn't just affect me."

"I understand, Sera. But you've sacrificed ten years of your life for them. Isn't it time to do something for you?"

Pulling her phone from her purse, she spent a couple of minutes searching for something. "My bus leaves in three hours. Maybe I should go pack."

"If that's what you want." Alex took her hand and waited until he had her full attention. "But I have one more place to take you."

SHE LOOKED UP at the sign. "A bar?"

Alex crossed his arms and nodded. "A hard cider bar."

Sera patted her belly. Memories of twenty-four hours earlier were still fresh. She wasn't about to push things. "I think I'll stick with ginger ale."

"Which is fine, but I wanted you to meet my friend Will. He owns the place." Alex led her into the establishment.

When they stood just inside, a broad-shouldered, bearded man behind the bar motioned to them. "Hey, you two. Corner table. I'll be there in a minute."

Alex led her to a red leather booth. He smiled as they both slid onto the seat. "That's the owner, Will. Remember the first time we met?"

She couldn't hold back the smile at the memory. "If not for Mike and his hard cider, you would have slept in the airport lobby that night."

Alex laughed. "I owe Mike. As a matter of fact, I thought I might introduce him to the owner here."

Sera blinked. Alex helping out one of the locals was the last thing she expected. "That's a great idea, Alex. Will could stock Mike's Flying Apple hard cider."

"I like connecting people with opportunities."

The man was full of surprises. She bit her lip. "Thank you for taking me to the library this morning. I've missed going there whenever I felt like it. The renovations in the Rose Reading Room were amazing. And the train system is so cute." She propped her chin in her palm and searched his face. "Do you really think I could go back to school? At my age?"

"Hi. I thought I'd find you here." Carrie slipped into the booth and settled next to Alex. "Hi, Sera. I'm Carrie. I work with Alex. Don't tell me Alex's cousin stood you up?" She waved at the owner and turned back with a swirl of perfect hair. "I hope Alex stepped in."

"He did." She was about to ask Carrie what she did when Will arrived with four bottles.

After introductions, Alex explained Sera was just getting over a case of food poisoning so Will exchanged her hard cider for a ginger ale. Then he took a seat on the bench beside Sera. She glanced across the table at Alex, deep in conversation with his colleague. Sitting with the trio of friends, Sera was reminded of her days in school, when whether or not to go out for drinks was the biggest decision she had to make. Could she go back to school? Could she find a place for Aunt Hope and Shawn to live in comfortably?

"Alex said your brother plays in Nashville. Is he with a band?" Her conversation with Alex over, Carrie was focused on Sera and took a sip of her cider.

"He's been with a variety of bands. No one you've heard of. He graduated high school three years ago and went straight there. I thought he should attend college, but he had other ideas."

"School's not for everyone." Will leaned both arms on the table and tilted his head toward Alex and Carrie. "I was halfway through the first year of law school with these two until I figured that out."

"He dropped out and spent the rest of the year backpacking through Europe." Carrie took another swig from her bottle. "Good for us, though. Now we have a place to hang out."

Will spoke to Sera with a grin. "My dad still gets mad when the subject comes up."

Sera thought of Alex's issues with his

father and then wondered what her father would think of her decisions over the last ten years. Glancing at her watch, she started when she noticed the time. "I have to go." She gave each of the three a smile. "I haven't enjoyed myself this much in a long time. But I should be on my way. I don't want to miss the bus."

"I'll walk with you." Alex elbowed Carrie to let him out of the booth.

"You don't have to." Sera scooted along the bench seat. If she had learned anything in the last hour, it was the clear picture of Alex's full life in the city and that his time in Bear Meadows was temporary. Any thoughts she had of something more were foolish.

Alex helped her stand. "Don't argue. Besides, we're taking a cab."

They said their goodbyes. Out on the street, Alex pointed to the corner. "We'll have better luck getting a cab on Houston."

There wasn't much chance to talk as the cab raced to Alex's apartment, where she threw her stuff into her suitcase, and then seemed to arrive at the bus terminal in no time. The bus for Harrisburg was already boarding. They moved away as passengers surged toward the open door of the bus bound for Interstate 80.

"Sera."

"Alex."

They both laughed.

Alex grabbed her arm and pulled her close. "I had a great time this weekend."

The heat moved up Sera's neck and onto her cheeks at the memories of her first night in the city in ages. "Playing nursemaid? I'm sure you've had better dates." She froze as the word left her lips. "Not that this was a date, I mean, Cyrus was supposed to…"

"Hey, Sera, calm down." He pulled her even closer, although the crowd seemed to have thinned. "As far as I'm concerned, this weekend was Cy's loss and my gain."

Her body seemed to move toward Alex's, as if her feet were on a magic carpet. "I think so, too."

"Just before Carrie interrupted us, you asked if I thought you could return to school at your age. Personally, I think anyone can return to school at any age. If the school accepts you into the program again, I think you'd be crazy not to accept." He leaned in so his lips were only inches from hers and lowered his voice to a whisper. "I hope you come back to the city." And then he kissed her. A proper goodbye kiss. Not a spur-of-the-moment, wish-he-would-stop-talking kiss.

Sera melted into his embrace. For all she knew, the bus had left the station and she didn't care. When the kiss ended, she looked up into soft brown eyes. "Tell your cousin to make me an offer."

CHAPTER TEN

"PASS THE JELLY." Aunt Hope sat opposite her at the kitchen table, her gaze focused on a piece of dry toast on a saucer.

"So you are speaking to me." Sera pushed the jar of grape jelly within reach of her great-aunt.

Hope scooped a clump of jelly from the jar and spread it on her toast. She cut the bread diagonally and then set the knife next to her plate. She took a bite, all the while avoiding looking at Sera.

"Then again, maybe not." Sera rose from her chair and retrieved the iced tea from the refrigerator. "That's your lunch? Toast and jelly?"

"So in addition to telling me where I should live, now you're telling me what I can and cannot eat."

Sera resisted the urge to slam the refrigerator door. "Just concerned about your health."

"You're too kind." Hope's words dripped with sarcasm, an emotion Sera was surprised to hear from her normally pleasant great-aunt.

She hated that tone of voice. "Aunt Hope, what else can I do?"

"Does Chance know about this?"

"Chance doesn't care about the farm. Besides, I have his power of attorney." She filled her glass with tea and put the pitcher within reach of her great-aunt.

"Your father always said you were a smart girl."

Sera shot her great-aunt a look. "He's too busy having fun in Nashville, going for the big time, just like Dad. Only I'm not Mom. I'm not content to stay here and plant and plow and pull weeds just so everybody else can get what they want."

"Chance would not agree. I know he wouldn't."

The screen door opened. "Did I hear

my name?" Chance stood in the open doorway, duffel bag over his shoulder and carrying his guitar.

Sera's mouth dropped open. "What are you doing here?"

"What? I can't come home to visit?" He dropped his duffel bag next to Rocky's dog bed and leaned the guitar case in the corner. Then he walked over to his aunt and kissed her on the cheek. "I didn't want to miss Cy's big Fourth of July party."

"You don't know how happy I am to see you." Aunt Hope rose and returned his kiss. She looked over her shoulder at Sera. "We have a lot to talk about."

Sera checked through the open door. There was no trace of a car. "How did you get here?"

"April dropped me off." Chance grabbed a glass from the cupboard.

"April Madison?" Sera couldn't believe her ears. Chance had been acting strangely lately. *But April Madison? The flight attendant?*

"Yep." Opening the refrigerator door, Chance stood staring at the contents. "You two don't eat much, do you?"

Hope walked over to the cupboard and withdrew a jar. "Here's some peanut butter. You always liked my grape jelly. We have homemade bread. All the fixin's for a PB and J."

"That'll hold me until we get to Cy's. He always has a big spread." Chance poured a glass of iced tea and settled onto Hope's vacated seat. He grabbed two slices of bread and then stopped. He glanced from one to the other with narrowed eyes. "What were you two talking about when I came in?"

"We can discuss that later." Sera gulped the rest of her tea and carried the empty glass to the sink.

"You better talk now." Aunt Hope settled into her rocking chair and crossed her arms. She set the rocker going back and forth while fixing Sera with a steely-eyed glare.

Sera propped both arms on the counter

and hung her head. Chance had the knack of showing up at the worst times. She faced her brother. "I've decided to sell to Cyrus Carter. Aunt Hope is not happy, but I'm at my wit's end."

Chance's face didn't change expression one bit at her announcement. He finished spreading peanut butter and jelly on the bread and then slapped the top slice onto the bottom. He took a big bite, chewed and swallowed before responding. "You didn't mention to me you had come to a decision."

"You've never been concerned before." Sera looked from Chance to Hope, whose gaze was fixed on her great-nephew.

Chance took his time again. Having another bite. Chewing, swallowing. "I know, but my name is on the deed, too."

Sera gritted her teeth while at the same time wondering what in the world was going on in her little brother's head. She noticed Aunt Hope was watching them both like a spectator at a prizefight. She now looked back at her brother. “I have your power of attorney.”

“I thought that only came into play if I wasn’t available.” Chance emptied half the glass of iced tea in one swallow and set it on the table with a clunk. He smiled. “I’m available.”

Sera’s skin broke out in goose bumps at her brother’s unexpected response. Unfortunately, he was right. But never in a million years did she think he would go against her decision. Then she remembered that this was the little brother who, unlike her, liked to take risks. She blew out a breath, willing herself to remain calm. “I don’t have the time to discuss this any further. You two can go over to the Carters’ for the picnic. I’ve got strawberries to pick. Talk to you later, Chance.” She walked out onto the porch. Nothing was ever simple at Last Chance Farm. Absolutely nothing.

ALEX SAT IN the passenger seat of Carrie’s father’s luxury SUV. Carrie was driving and Will was in the back seat. When Alex had told his friends his experiences with trying to rent a car in Bear Meadows, the two had practically rolled on the floor with laughter. Then Carrie offered to drive the three of them to his cousin's Fourth of July picnic. Always invited as friends of Alex, she had wanted to come for years.

As they rode smoothly down Interstate 80, Alex fought the feeling of unease in the pit of his stomach. His mother had been thrilled when he told her he was going to be in the area for two weeks working on the theater mall project. As usual, she hadn't mentioned his father. He fully expected to see both parents at the annual picnic. Maybe he could avoid his father.

When they pulled into Clover Hill Farms, Alex hardly recognized the place. This year Cy had gone all out. Multiple grills were lined up along one side of the huge yard, delicious smells pouring out of each of them. A bar was arranged on the patio, the bartender busy tending to a line of people. Parking next to a line of vehicles in the recently cut hay field, the three of them got out and walked toward the house.

"Hey, you made it. I haven't seen you two since Alex's graduation party." Cy waved a spatula at them from the end grill. Flames shot up through the grates, searing the hamburgers on the surface. Pointing to his apron that said Kiss the Cook, he gave Carrie a wink. When she kissed him on the cheek, he groaned. "Is that all I get?"

Carrie laughed.

Alex greeted his cousin with a quick pat on the back, glad Cy was in a good mood. Sera's decision probably had a lot to do with it. "Hey, how are you?"

"Great." Cy tilted his head toward the house. "Your mom is in the kitchen."

"I better say hello." He spotted Mike from the airport. "Will, I want to introduce you to this guy."

He left Will, Carrie and Mike talking

about cider brands and strolled past the temporary bar. He was smiling when he opened the kitchen door, expecting to see his mother. But the first person he saw was his father. He swallowed and pasted on a smile. Sera said the Callahans buried their feelings. Well, the Kimmels could pretend with the best of them. "Hi, Dad."

Max gave his son a long look and simply grunted in response.

Ignoring the sound, Alex wrapped his arms around his mother and squeezed. "Hi, Mom."

"Hi, sweetie." She patted his face. "I'm so glad you're here."

"Hello, Aunt Hope, Aunt Jean, Uncle Bob." From the looks they gave him, Alex had the feeling he had been the topic of conversation around the table.

"Be careful, Jean." Max resumed his seat at the head of the table. "My son, Alex, has a tendency to throw old people out of their homes."

"Dad." Alex's hands automatically

flexed, and he resisted the urge to flee. "It wasn't like that."

"You were interviewed on national news. Sure came across that way."

"I didn't displace them." Alex looked out the kitchen door at Will and Carrie having fun talking to Cy and Mike. He never should have come into the house. He faced his father. "They moved into fine nursing homes. The husband needed special care." He glanced through the door again, wondering if Sera were out there somewhere.

"That's right. That's why you should've left them alone."

He needed to see Sera. "We needed the property."

"All about money with you, isn't it? Nice job, Alex."

SHE WAITED UNTIL almost dusk before giving in to her grumbling stomach. Chance was right. There was nothing in the house to eat but peanut butter and jelly. He had eaten all the bread but a piece of crust.

Since he had commandeered the truck, she drove the golf cart along the edge of the road to Cy's. Feeling silly showing up in the retrofitted golf cart, she parked in front of the house and walked around back.

The first person Sera saw was Alex. He was leaning against a tree, staring at the brown bottle in his hand.

"Long time no see."

Her words brought a smile to his face. "Sera. I didn't think you were coming."

She took the bottle from his hand and took a sip, then handed it back. "I wasn't going to, but we don't have any food in the house and I'm starving."

"Let's go get you a plate. I'm a little hungry now, myself."

As she chose potato salad, baked beans and an unrecognizable cheesy dish that may have had broccoli in it, and grabbed a hamburger, she observed Will and Carrie deep in conversation with Mike, the airport bartender. She motioned to Alex. "You did it."

He grinned. "I did. Let's go sit over here." He led her to a bench half hidden under a giant oak tree.

"Who's that?" Alex pointed toward the patio.

Sera had been so busy concentrating on balancing her plate and cup that she hadn't noticed any of the other visitors. She looked up.

The sight of Chance, sitting on the patio strumming his guitar, surrounded by a trio of women, shouldn't have surprised her. "That is my baby brother."

Alex's eyebrows rose. "That's Chance?"

She nodded. "Not what you expected?"

"I don't know." He set his empty plate on the grass. "I guess I thought he'd be more like you. He looks kind of…"

"Flashy?"

"Something like that." Alex gave her a steady look. "Your brother must attract quite the following in Nashville."

"I really don't know. He doesn't share much of his life with me. I do know that Nashville is full of guys just like him.

Whether he has what it takes to rise to the top remains to be seen."

"Cy looks happy. You must have given him the good news." He rested against the bench and stretched his arm along the back behind her.

Sera leaned into him. It seemed like the most natural thing in the world. "I did and he is."

"How is Hope taking it?" Alex brushed a strand of hair from her face.

"Not well."

"I'm sorry to hear that. I saw her briefly earlier. She was in the kitchen with the older folk, including my dad. He took it upon himself to inform everyone my specialty is throwing old people out of their homes."

"Ouch."

"I don't think I'm on your great-aunt's good side anymore."

"Join the club." Despite the festive atmosphere, Sera was having a hard time getting in a party mood. From the sounds of things, so was Alex.

"Earth to Sera." She felt a tap on her shoulder. "What are your plans?"

"The Hunters are selling their house in town. It's on the same street as Hope's friend Mrs. Hershberger."

"So you'll stay in the area."

"It's either that or move her into the nursing home in town. Don't tell my great-aunt, but I did take a tour. You know, come to think of it, I saw that they have staff trained for all sorts of conditions."

"So?"

"Your couple, the one that was separated..."

"Don't remind me."

"They were separated because the facility didn't accept patients with dementia, right?"

"Thanks for thinking of me, but their extended family all live down east. I doubt they'd want to move up here."

"The company that owns the nursing home in town has multiple locations. Maybe they have a place where they could both go. Your dad wouldn't have anything to bug you about."

He chuckled. "Yes, he would. He's still mad I didn't come home and work for him."

"Well, you can't have it all, can you?"

"What will you do?" Taking her plate, he set it on the grass next to his.

"Maybe take some classes at Penn State. I can commute from home."

"What about Nomi's offer?"

She jerked her gaze from the party guests to Alex. "You knew she got the scholarship reinstated?"

"Nomi texted me." He took both her hands in his. "You would be close to the city again."

Sera squeezed his fingers. "But what about Hope and Shawn?"

"What about you, Sera?" He leaned closer.

Sera's breath grew short. She stared into the brown eyes, trying to interpret his question. Was he asking what she thought he was asking?

"Sera! Hey, did you try the pulled pork?" Cy dipped his head to miss the lower branches of the big tree. Sera pulled her hands from Alex's and picked up her plate.

She turned to Cy. "Not yet. I was headed over there, though."

Cy looked from Sera to Alex and back again. "By the way, I wanted to apologize for leaving you stranded in New York. Lucky for me Alex was able to step in. We'll reschedule, okay?"

"Maybe." Sera glanced at Alex, wondering if he had told his cousin about moving her to his apartment. Alex was stabbing macaroni salad with a plastic fork.

"I'll pay. You'll be out from under the farm, so you should be doing better." He again looked from one to the other. "How'd your great-aunt take the news?"

"Not well."

"I was afraid of that. She'll get over it."

Sera shot him a glance, irritated at the

offhand remark. "Last Chance Farm has been her only home, Cy."

"I know. I didn't mean that the way it sounded." He took her empty plate from her hands. "I have a favor to ask. Alex was supposed to stay here for a couple weeks while he works in the area but I'm renovating the upstairs. Can he stay with you?"

"Again? Cy, you're taking advantage." Alex stood.

"I'll give you some cash for rent. It'll work out for both of us. He can help you gather up the necessary papers. I'll come over tomorrow afternoon. We can tie up the loose ends."

Sera flashed on her brother's surprise return, the smile he had given her when he said he was available, that she no longer needed the power of attorney. Before, he had flown in and flown out, visiting friends, making connections, with hardly a word for her or Hope. Suddenly he's available? Something was definitely up with her little brother. Tying up loose ends might be a problem.

"WAS I MISTAKEN, or do I see a little spark between you and the lovely Sera?" Carrie hooked Alex's arm as he passed by. Sera had accompanied Cy in search of the pulled pork.

"What? Oh, no, of course not." Alex thought he and Sera had been well hidden on the bench, but he should have known the sharp-eyed Carrie would notice.

"Why not? She's pretty, she's smart. She would be good for you."

"How do you figure?"

"She would remind you life's not all about work."

"Look who's talking."

Alex's mother came up to them. "Carrie, it's been a long time. So nice that you could come."

"Will's here, too." She pointed to where Will and Mike sat in the grass listening to Chance play guitar.

"We haven't seen you two since law school graduation."

"When you stole Alex away from us with the promise of bright lights and fast cars." Max appeared behind his wife.

Alex groaned. "Dad..."

But Carrie only laughed. "Bright lights, maybe, Mr. Kimmel, but your son and cars do not mix. It's a good thing we have public transportation in the city."

"We were just leaving. Excuse us." Beverly tugged on Max's elbow and steered him toward the line of cars. Alex guessed his father was in for a lecture of his own.

"We should head back, too." Carrie gave him a sympathetic look.

"So soon?" Cy approached with Sera, who was deep in conversation with her brother.

Slinging the guitar to his back, Chance gave Alex a wide smile. "So, you're Cy's cousin. The lawyer from New York."

"Alex." He reached out to shake hands.

Chance seemed to hesitate before shaking hands. "Chance Callahan."

Alex winced. The guitar player had a strong grip. "You're the country Western singer from Nashville."

"I currently reside in Nashville, but I'm from Bear Meadows, just like my big sister. In fact, Last Chance Farm is technically half mine." He tilted his head and a curly lock of dark hair fell over his forehead. He flashed a smile. "Did you know that?"

"I heard." Alex had a feeling that the ready smile was a technique the singer was accustomed to using.

"You're the one who talked my sister into selling to Cy. I've haven't seen any numbers yet, but I'll lay odds Cy is getting a good deal."

Alex's muscles tensed at the man's implications. "Now, wait just a minute…" Bad enough his own father accused him of putting money before people. But this kid?

Still smiling, Chance held up a hand.

"Just sayin', my man, just sayin'. Now if you'll excuse me, I should get Aunt Hope back…home." He emphasized the last word and then strutted across the yard, the eyes of several females following his every move. From the excited voices as he entered the kitchen, Alex figured Chance was as popular with the older generation as he was with the younger.

He felt a tug on the back of his shirt. Sera stood behind him, her eyes darting from him to Carrie and Cy, who were talking. "Ready to go?"

"Am I staying with you? I don't think your brother would approve." At his words, Chance emerged from the kitchen and helped his great-aunt down the steps. "Or your great-aunt, for that matter."

"He'll take Aunt Hope home and then come back here to party. Trust me, I know my brother. He's a night owl."

"Then maybe I should go back to your place, although no doubt Chance will make me sit in back and go over potholes on purpose, hoping to bounce me off into a ditch. Hey, wait a minute. You two do have some similarities."

His words brought a chuckle and a slap on the arm.

"I happen to have the best seat in the house for Cy's fireworks," she told him.

He looked down into twinkling eyes that were the color of the Caribbean Sea. At this point, he would go anywhere with her. "Where?"

Sera reached for his hand and pulled him into the shadows at the side of the house. "On top of the hill in my apple orchard. Just the two of us."

CHAPTER ELEVEN

"WHAT ARE YOU DOING?"

Standing at the bookcase in the front room, Chance rifled through the shelves. "Just looking around. Do you know where Mom kept our baby books?"

"No clue. Why?" Sera walked into the room and checked out their mother's desk. Still messy.

"Just wanted to see how cute I was as a baby." He smiled, but his attention was still on the bookcase. In cutoff jeans and a T-shirt, he looked exactly as he had in high school. Except for the two-day growth of dark beard.

"You must be going into adoration withdrawal. You better fly south as soon as possible."

Chance closed a book and returned it to a shelf. “I needed a break.”

“Can I help you find something?” Alex entered the room. He was wearing khakis and a checked shirt.

Chance frowned. “You’re staying here?” He looked at his sister. “Why is he here?”

“Chance, please. You’re being rude. Cy asked if he could stay here while he’s renovating.” The night before, she and Alex had ridden the golf cart past the house and up to the apple orchard, where they had a perfect view of Cy’s fireworks display. And no distracting relatives.

“Sera, you are so naive. The man is appraising the property for his cousin. You’re giving him access to everything.”

Alex came and stood beside her. “I’m not taking advantage of anyone.”

Sera held up her hands like a traffic cop. “He’s cleaning up a mess of legal papers that have been all over the house for ten years. I certainly haven’t had time. Besides, he’s paying rent.”

Taking a seat on the sofa, Chance gave them both a long look. "Rent. He's paying you rent? How convenient."

Sera wasn't sure what had happened in less than twelve hours to make the two men so antagonistic toward one another. "I came to tell you lunch is ready. Aunt Hope made lasagna just for you, Chance." She poked him in the chest with her finger. Maybe feeding the two men would put them in a better mood.

Chance smiled as he tried to grab her finger. "Because I'm her favorite."

"We're eating in the dining room." She led the way down the hall and into the first room off the kitchen. She came to a stop in the doorway. "Hi, Shawn. I didn't realize you were coming over for lunch."

"Your great-aunt invited me." He handed Sera a bag. "I brought you two some candy from the new store in town. I know you like chocolate."

Sera peeked into the bag stuffed with a variety of confections. Puzzled, she glanced at her hired hand. "This must've cost a fortune, Shawn. You shouldn't have."

He shrugged. "It's the least I can do. I appreciate sharing a meal with the family. I hope you don't mind." His gaze zeroed in on Alex, coming in behind her. "I'm Shawn Murphy, young man. And who might you be?" His round face bore half a smile.

"Alex Kimmel." Alex returned the grin, which led Sera to wonder if the two men already knew each other. She shook it off. With Chance's surprise return home, she had enough to think about without inventing another conspiracy.

"Pleased to make your acquaintance." He gave a nod to Aunt Hope, who had set a large dish of steaming lasagna at one end of the table and was ladling out chunks with a spatula.

She gave Sera a look. "Been a while since we ate in the dining room. I thought we could use the extra space. Nice to have the family together again." Her gaze paused on Alex. “And of course company is always welcome.”

Sera glanced from Chance to her great-aunt to Shawn, about to point out Shawn wasn’t family, either, but she didn’t want to hurt the older man’s feelings. Instead, she motioned to Alex to sit, and she took the chair next to him, her growling stomach reminding her all she had so far that day was coffee. “This smells wonderful, Aunt Hope. It’s been a while.”

Aunt Hope returned her smile. “It’s been a while since I’ve had anyone to cook for.”

Forking off a bite of the Italian dish, the mozzarella stretched in a long string from the plate to her mouth. Her great-aunt was right. Between the two of them, they barely ate enough to make cooking a formal meal worthwhile. So they had gotten in the habit of just picking. Sera looked around the table.

“Salad, garlic bread… Thanks for coming, guys.” Sera smiled, happy for the first time in a long time. So what if she didn't know why Chance was home? He had a weird schedule. And Shawn had been around so long he was almost family. As for Alex… "I hope you were hungry."

He nodded, before turning to the woman at the end of the table. "This is delicious. Thanks for including me."

"Where'd you run off to last night, sis? Cy was looking everywhere for you. Pass that last slice of garlic bread." Chance reached out for the basket. He was already on his second helping of lasagna.

Handing him the bread, Sera was curious as to what would've prompted her brother's question. She searched the green eyes so similar to hers for a clue. "When I left he was deep in conversation with Dr. Hannah. I think he's interested."

"I thought he was interested in you."

"He's interested in the farm, not me."

"But you two used to date."

"We went to the prom. No big deal." Finishing the last bite on her plate, Sera stood and took her plate into the kitchen.

When she returned, she acted as if she had forgotten Chance's comment. "Cy is coming over in an hour. Are you finished?" She reached for Chance's plate.

He put his hand over hers. "Can we talk a minute?"

"Good idea. Let's clear the table first." Belying her ninety-some years, Aunt Hope jumped up. Chance carried the dishes and then returned to the table. He gave Alex a pointed look. "Would you excuse us, Alex?" He smiled. "Family business."

Alex looked down at the half-finished meal on his plate. "Sure. I should get started on those papers in the den." Balancing his plate, silverware and glass, Alex disappeared into the hall.

"Finally," Chance muttered.

"You're impossible." Sera shook her head. "What do you have against Alex?"

"Other than he's an attorney from the city? Nothing. I would think you'd've learned your lesson."

"I should go, too." Shawn stood. He

patted his stomach. “Thank you all for lunch.”

“Shawn, you don’t have to go.” Aunt Hope’s look was hopeful.

He took her hand. “I do. Thank you again.” He disappeared.

Sera dabbed at crumbs on the white tablecloth, trying in vain to interpret the undercurrents in the house since Chance had shown up. He certainly didn’t like Alex being around. But surely he didn’t want to talk about the sale of the farm. Unless he was worried they weren’t getting enough money.

“So, what’s up?” She folded her arms and leaned forward to rest on the table. At Chance’s smile, a shiver of excitement gave her goose bumps. “Do you have news to share?” That had to be it. “Dad always said you were talented. What is it? Blue Bird Café? Grand Ole Opry?”

Chance smiled but shook his head. “I have news, though not on the music front.”

“A record deal. You’re kidding. You got

a record deal?" Sera pounded the table with her fist, causing the salt shaker to fall over.

"Sit, sis. You're not listening. No, it's none of the above." He folded his napkin carefully. "Last spring, I met a girl."

She righted the salt shaker. A feeling of unease came over her. "You--"

Chance held up one hand. "Hold on. As I was saying, I met a girl."

Sera sat back in her chair. Her chest constricted. Surely Chance wasn't moving home with somebody he just met. She looked at Hope, who sat quietly observing her great-nephew.

"Annabelle was a trainer who worked with racehorses in Kentucky. Last spring she was in Nashville for a month, working with the horses of one of the country singers."

"You're speaking in the past tense, so it must be over. Why are you telling us this? You go through girlfriends like tissues."

Rolling his eyes, Chance continued as if she hadn't spoken, "We were together all month, then she went back to Kentucky. We texted a couple times, then she stopped and I figured she was busy with her life and I was busy so…"

The sexy smile was gone. Chance ran his finger down the crease of the napkin. In the kitchen, Rocky growled, probably dreaming. She rubbed the goose bumps suddenly on her arms and found herself growing angry. "Chance, if you…"

"Let him talk, Sera. He has just as much right as you."

Sera bit the inside of her cheek. Everybody had rights, but she was the one who provided all those rights. The right for Chance to follow his dream, the right for Hope to live out her life at home…

"A couple weeks ago the owners of the Kentucky farm where she worked looked me up. J.R. and Betsy Conrad. They own Fast Track Farms." He folded the paper napkin into even tinier squares. "They told me Anna had a baby. About six months ago."

Sera's lips tightened. "Why would they tell you?"

His smile was back. Not the sexy smile. This one was different. "Because I'm the father."

"No, no, no." With a groan to rival Rocky's, Sera lay her head on her arms, resting on the table. Then she shot her brother a look. "Why didn't Anna come tell you?"

He dropped his chin to his chest and rubbed the inner corners of his eyes with his thumb and forefinger. Then he took a deep breath. "She had a pulmonary embolism during childbirth. She died."

"Oh, no." Aunt Hope's hands flew to her mouth.

Sera sank into her chair and returned her brother's gaze.

"They've been raising the baby. They didn't know about me until recently."

She slapped a hand on the tablecloth, causing Hope to jump in alarm. "They want child support. Oh, man, Chance, you can't even afford rent. How can you pay child support?"

He shook his head, curly hair flopping in all directions. "No, they don't want child support, Sera."

Aunt Hope's voice was soft. "They want you to raise your child. To bring your child home."

Sera couldn't help but feel Aunt Hope's tone bore a note of triumph. Her head dropped into her hands. What else could go wrong today?

A voice boomed from the kitchen. "Sorry I'm late. The cows got out."

Sera raised her eyes. Cyrus Carter stood in the doorway to the dining room, a big smile on his face and his hat in his hand.

He beamed at her. "Ready to go over those figures?"

CHAPTER TWELVE

THE FIRST THOUGHT in her mind when she woke Monday morning was that somewhere in Kentucky she had a niece. The second thought she had was one more mouth to feed. And she would continue to work her tail off. Cyrus had not been happy when she told him the negotiations would have to be postponed. Alex had made himself scarce.

She wasn't sure what Chance wanted to do. The announcement had been so shocking. Chance said he wasn't sure.

A knock sounded on her door. "Are you decent?"

"Come in."

Chance came in and sat on the edge of the bed. "You must be disappointed in me."

"I'm not disappointed. I'm just…worried."

"What do you think I should do?"

"I have no idea. I mean, you would be a single father, and you work such a strange schedule. I mean, remember what it was like with Dad? He was never home."

He hung his head. "You're right."

Resting a hand on his shoulder, she looked him in the eyes. "We have a lot to talk about. And I shouldn't make any big decisions before caffeine. I'll meet you downstairs."

Ten minutes later she joined her brother in the kitchen. Aunt Hope stood at the stove flipping pancakes. Sera poured coffee into her favorite mug. "You're full of energy this morning."

"The idea of a baby in the house makes me feel young again."

Sera's stomach flipped. She exchanged a glance with her brother, who sat in Hope's rocking chair next to Lucky. "I don't think Chance has decided what he's going to do yet."

"What's to decide? Bring the child home where she belongs. He's the baby daddy. Nobody cares about single parents anymore."

Sera stared at her great-aunt in shock but bit her tongue. She turned and stared out the back door. The tomatoes in the garden were dark green and healthy looking. That was good news. The corn was knee-high. Good news again. "I am in the garden from dawn to dusk, Hope. You're too—" She stopped when her great-aunt glared. "Too out of practice to care for a baby."

"Sera's right, Aunt Hope." Chance came over and stood next to the woman at the stove. "I can't ask either of you to take this on. It's my problem."

"Nonsense. We're family. That's what we do. We take care of each other."

She turned and poked a bony finger in her nephew's chest. "I know what I'm talking about. If you leave that child with strangers, you'll regret it for the rest of your life."

Sera shook her head. Her great-aunt had never left the farm. What did she know? "What if giving the baby up provides her with a better life?"

"Then that would be different." She waved her hand around like the queen in a parade. "But look at this place. What better place to raise a child than here at Last Chance Farm?"

Chance looked at his sister. "Then I'll move back home."

"You have a career to think about." Aunt Hope flipped a pancake with practiced ease.

Sera was unable to believe what she was proposing. She took Chance's seat in the rocker, going back and forth, back and forth.

Chance carried the plates with food his great-aunt handed to him and set them on the table. He and Hope sat and then looked at Sera, who remained rocking. "You go any faster in that thing, you're going to fly out the door. What's on your mind?"

Sera stopped the rocker with one foot.

Her head was swimming, whether from the rocking or the news she wasn't sure. "Let me get this straight. You and Aunt Hope agree you should raise your child and you and Aunt Hope agree you should continue your career. Exactly how do those two goals work?" She crossed her arms tight against her chest and waited for one or both of her remaining family to solve the problem. And as had been the tradition for the last ten years, neither had an answer. They turned to their plates and drowned the pancakes with syrup.

"SMART OF YOU to avoid the kitchen this morning." Sera set a steaming cup of coffee on the clean desk surface. "I figured you could use this."

"Thanks."

"I can handle Aunt Hope on her own. And I can handle Chance on his own. But together? They're a formidable force."

"They don't want you to sell."

Curled up in the Queen Anne chair, she shook her head. "The baby is the next generation of Callahans. Aunt Hope is over the moon."

"I thought she'd be unhappy with the circumstances."

"Surprisingly no."

"Well..." Alex leaned back in the desk chair and pointed at the clean desk surface. "Every scrap of paper is filed in its proper folder."

"Every scrap?"

"Every scrap. I was afraid to throw anything out. Your mother had a lot of notes about her crops." He pointed to the desk. "Lower left drawer." He raised his eyes to hers. "In case you change your mind."

"Do you think Cy will ever speak to me again?"

"To borrow one of his sayings, he'll get over it. The question is, what about you?"

"Me? I keep doing what I'm doing. If Chance decides to stay, maybe we can increase production."

"Chance is giving up Nashville?" Alex pictured the young man sitting on the picnic table strumming his guitar surrounded by adoring fans.

Sera's eyebrows shot upward. "Yet to be determined. He wants to have his cake and eat it, too." Her shoulders drooped. "Of course, don't we all?"

"So you've changed your mind about selling to Cy?"

Alex drummed his fingers against the smooth surface of the old desk. Sera had been talking about Chance and Hope, but Alex couldn't help but think about his cousin, who also wanted it all. All of Last Chance Farm.

"WHAT ARE WE going to do?"

Sera inspected the underside of a tomato leaf for insect infestations. "We?" She straightened and pressed her hands to the small of her back, trying to stretch out the constant ache from bending over the plants. "I thought you and Hope had all the answers."

"Come on, Sera, this is serious."

"Are you staying or are you going?"

Chance looked out across the fields and sighed. "I guess I'm staying."

"With the baby."

"I'll drive down to Nashville and bring the baby back home."

"We don't have a car."

"Oh, right. Then I guess I'll fly down and rent a car."

Sera was sure she saw dollar signs flying through the air and up into the sky. "We'll have to increase revenue. We're barely getting by."

"Maybe I can sing, do shows."

"In Bear Meadows?"

"Sure, why not?"

"I'm not sure how much you'll get paid."

"Well, then, we'll just find as many ways to make money this year as we can. Those apples by the cabin, for instance. They must be good for something. Why else did Mom plant them?"

"Good question. I don't have the answer. She must've made a mistake." Sera stared at the ridgetops in the distance, covered in varying shades of green from oaks and maples and pines. "I do have another idea, but I'll need some help."

"What's that?"

"Believe it or not, a young couple from the area want to get married in our barn. Originally I said no. But what do I care if the barn is dusty and full of cobwebs? It's not my wedding, right?" Sera knelt in the soil and continued to inspect her plants.

Chance propped his hands on his hips and threw back his shoulders. "That's a great idea."

She looked up at her handsome brother, his dark hair ruffled by the breeze, his scruffy beard giving him an air of adventure, and his blue-green eyes twinkling with excitement. "Glad you agree." She felt a sense of relief. Maybe he was finally ready to lend a necessary hand.

"Sure, that's right up my alley. I can sing at the wedding."

Sera stared at the dirt. *That's what he got out of the conversation?* But before she could ask him, he continued.

"Would you take me to the airport? There's a flight out this afternoon. We can't afford for me to waste another minute."

CHAPTER THIRTEEN

"ARE YOU STILL INTERESTED?" Sera looked from Josh to Wendy.

Wendy looked at her sister. "What do you think, Katie?"

The New York reporter walked slowly around the barn. "We only have two months. The yard wedding would be easier."

"But a barn wedding is friendlier." Wendy wrapped her hand around Josh's arm. Her diamond glittered in the sun. "It's more us. You can have the backyard wedding."

Her sister scoffed. "Unlikely to ever happen, little sis."

Throwing back her shoulders, Wendy gave all three of them a look of resolve. "I want a harvest moon wedding."

"Harvest moon. I'm guessing that's in the fall." Katie's tone was dry.

"The full moon closest to the autumnal equinox."

Josh stared at the birds flying among the rafters. He looked doubtful. "Leave it to a weather person to know that."

"Former weather person."

Sera marveled at the sisters' differences. Katie was tall and willowy with dark blond hair. Wendy was of average height with sleek almost-black hair. But the sisters had the same oval face and high cheekbones and what one might call a television personality. She had hoped the entire family would have come at her call, but the parents were on a cruise to Bermuda. "Your father offered to hire a painter." Sera almost cringed when she brought up the subject, but she certainly couldn't afford to hire a painter, and if the couple could afford a cruise…

Panning the entire scope of the barn with her beautiful blue eyes, Katie nodded. "The barn certainly needs some work, doesn't it?" Her gaze landed on her sister.

Sera should've jumped at Bernie Valentine's offer. Fathers of brides would agree to anything. Now she was dealing with this savvy New Yorker. With Chance's bombshell announcement, she was desperate for this wedding to take place.

"Dad did say that, Katie." Wendy's smile spoke volumes. She was already convinced.

"Did he?" Katie continued to stroll around the barn. She stopped when she came to the three square holes in the floor.

Sera went and joined her. Down below she could see the kittens playing in the hay. "That's where we used to throw hay down to the animals."

Katie nodded and looked at her. "They'll need to be covered. Holes in floors are a hazard at weddings."

"Of course." Sera wrung her hands. She should've waited for Bernie and Babs. She looked at Josh and Wendy, who were watching Katie critique the space. She needed to distract them from all the things wrong with the barn. "So how did you two meet?"

With a sly smile, Josh eyed his fiancé. "I saved her life."

"You did not." Wendy slapped him on the arm. "I was stuck in a snowdrift and Josh happened to come along." She grinned at him, and suddenly the conversation seemed to be a silent communication between the two of them.

Katie joined them. "I do know a wedding planner."

"Do you think she'd come out here?" Wendy gripped Josh's arm so tightly he winced.

"For me, she would." Katie smiled. "I'll make a call. We have a wedding to arrange."

"ASK AUNT JEAN if I can borrow her car." Alex shifted in the desk chair. Now that the loose papers were filed away, he could see the desk was really a beautiful piece of furniture.

"I've heard you're hard on vehicles." Cy grunted. Alex had obviously caught him in the middle of doing some farm-related task. "Okay, I'm sure she'll loan you the car. But what about the farm? Has Chance completely upset things over there?"

"You don't even want to know." Alex didn't want to be the one to spread the word of Chance's latest news. "Besides, isn't one farm enough? Short of marrying her, I think you should forget about owning this farm. Just be happy she rents you her fields." He held the phone away from his ear as Cy expressed his frustration, whether at the news or the task, he wasn't entirely sure. "If Sera can give me a ride, I'll be over in an hour." Alex clicked off his phone. Cy was still cursing.

He looked at the computer sitting on the corner of the desk and checked the website. Sera had been right. The owners of the nursing home in Bear Meadows owned several in the eastern half of Pennsylvania, as well. Maybe he could make amends after all. Right now, he needed to find Sera. He needed a ride.

"I'M OFF TO pick up your great-great-niece." Sera stood at the entrance to the bedroom that had been a playroom for her and Chance. Lucky the old house had six bedrooms. They were rapidly filling up.

Hope draped a familiar-looking baby quilt over the railing of a crib. "Look at this crib. Mac McAndrews brought it out. We have such good people in this town." Chance had only been gone a week. Aunt Hope had been busy burning up the phone lines.

"Doesn't he need it?"

"Apparently their little boy has graduated to a toddler bed."

"Is that Chance's quilt?" She ran a finger along the tiny stitches. "I thought he destroyed it. He was always chewing on the corner."

"I repaired it. I hoped one day we

would use it." She smiled. "And that day has finally come. Although I have to admit, I thought we would be filling this room with one of your babies before Chance's. But who am I to question the ways of the world?"

Sera gritted her teeth, wondering how she could have a baby without a husband and how to get a husband without a boyfriend and how to get a boyfriend without dating and how... "Listen, why don't you take a break? You don't want to overdo it."

"I feel wonderful." She grabbed a dust cloth and went to work on the wooden rocking chair next to the window. "Mac's deputy, Moose Williams, is loaning us their crib, too."

Sera pictured the house filling with used baby furniture. "Why do we need two cribs?"

Hope stopped what she was doing and looked at her as if the answer would be obvious to anyone. "So we have one upstairs and one downstairs."

Sera shook her head. The baby was Hope and Chance's project. "Have fun. I'm off to the airport." She ran down the stairs and through the hall. She stopped when she saw Alex working at the desk. "Not going out today?"

Alex looked up. "As a matter of fact. Aunt Jean is loaning me her car. Can you give me a ride?"

She looked at her watch. "I'm picking up my brother—" she moved farther into the room "— and my niece."

Alex sat back in his chair and steepled his fingers under his chin. "A baby." He shook his head. "Wow. A lot of responsibility."

"You're upset I changed my mind about selling to your cousin."

"Me? Heck, no. I don't care about my cousin. Well, I care, but not about whether he gets your property. I'm just concerned. You already have a lot on your plate."

"My brother will take care of the baby. Nothing really changes."

"You think so?"

"Listen, Alex, no offense, but this is family business."

"Is this one of those things we're never to speak of again?"

Sera's insides curled at his reminder of her impetuous act the night of the rainstorm. She turned and threw her goodbye over her shoulder. "If you want a ride, I'm leaving right now." Behind her she heard the desk chair hit the bookcase. She smiled.

An hour later she left Old Blue in short-term parking and walked into the airport lobby. The first person she saw was Al, probably on his way to the ramp to unload baggage.

In the waiting area, she watched the passengers walk down the stairs onto the ramp. Two college students, their Penn State attire loudly proclaiming their allegiance, a middle-aged woman with a big purse, an older man. The stairs emptied, as did the luggage cart next to the plane. April, the flight attendant, appeared at the top of the stairs and then just as quickly disappeared.

Sera's breath grew short, concerned her little brother had missed the plane. Had something gone wrong? Did the Conrads change their minds? Did the baby get sick? She was about to turn away when a form emerged from the plane.

Chance Callahan stood at the top of the stairs, his thick, wavy hair blowing in the slight breeze. In his arms he held a baby, her matching dark curls blowing in the same breeze. She wore denim bib overalls and a pink ruffled shirt. Sera was sure, with the long hair, the two-day beard and now a baby, her little brother was more of a chick magnet than ever. And as if to confirm her thoughts, April Madison re-appeared in the plane's doorway carrying a checkered diaper bag. Chance started down the stairs, the child clutched in his arms, followed by April.

Sera's heart went out to the two people coming toward her. The younger brother she had rocked to sleep after they lost their parents and the motherless little girl who was depending on Chance to provide her with family.

Life had thrown Sera another curveball. Nothing would ever be the same.

CHAPTER FOURTEEN

THE NEW YORK contingent didn't waste any time. Since Josh and Wendy were in South Dakota doing a story on the Crazy Horse monument, Katie Valentine took charge of the wedding project as if she remodeled barns every day. The event planner had arrived the day before.

Walking up to the barn, Sera passed Katie's black SUV, Jean Carter's sedan, on loan to Alex, the van belonging to the painter and finally the pickup with the large pressure washer in the bed. Ten years with just her, Hope and Shawn, and suddenly there were people popping up all over the place. How had that happened?

Chance and the baby had settled into a sort of routine. He would bathe and dress the baby in the morning, then bring her down to the kitchen for Aunt Hope to feed in the high chair while he worked on his music in the den. Despite her hopes, Chance had yet to take up any of the slack around the farm. It had been only two weeks. He was still learning to be a dad.

Katie Valentine paced in the open doorway of the barn. “Good morning, Sera.”

“Good morning, Katie. You’re up early.”

“This hiatus from my show is starting to lose its shine. I really needed this. It’s something to keep busy.” She pointed to a young woman on the other side of the barn. “Let me introduce you to Kristen.”

Sera was shocked. She had expected a much older woman, but Kristen Rose looked to be her own age. With light brown hair pulled back in a ponytail, the woman still managed to look elegant in jeans, a simple top and sneakers. “Nice to meet you, Kristen. I’m surprised you agreed to come way out here for a wedding.”

Kristen looped her arm through Katie's. "This woman was a big help to me when I got into the business. I'm happy to return the favor."

Katie patted her hand. "We're going to have so much fun at this wedding, Sera."

Sera shook her head. "Oh, I won't be going. I'll stay out of the way when the big day arrives."

"But of course you're going. This is your entrance into the events world."

"Even if I wanted to go, I have nothing in my closet."

Katie looked her up and down. "You and I are about the same size. I have the perfect dress for you. It'll bring out those turquoise eyes."

Before Sera could object, a deep voice bellowed from behind. "Where are we starting, ladies?" The man in well-worn overalls patted the machine sitting beside him in the doorway. "We're ready to go to work."

Sera approached and from the corner of her eye noticed Cy's shiny truck parked behind his mother's sedan. She turned to Kristen. "Are you sorry you agreed to this project?"

The woman from New York shook her head, sending her ponytail flying. "Are you kidding? Your barn is a blank canvas. You won't recognize the place when I'm done with it."

Sera backed away as the man with the pressure washer pulled hoses across the barn floor. "I never thought of using my barn for income. Up until last week I was selling the place."

"Your home?"

"You wouldn't believe the expense involved in operating a farm like this."

Kristen surveyed the space before her. "You must have heard, the average millionaire has seven streams of income." She made the comment as if it were something everybody knew.

"I'm no millionaire."

"What I'm saying is, you don't have to rely on just one source. I noticed your huge garden. You must sell vegetables.

That's one stream." She waved a hand around the barn. "This is a second."

"Two streams of income." Sera skimmed the interior of the barn, suddenly seeing it with new eyes. "I do rent out my fields."

Kristen nodded. "Three streams. You're on your way. And you know, organic vegetables are in high demand. You just have to be a certified organic grower."

"Certified?" Sera smiled, her heart actually lightened by the event planner's observations. "Well. What do you know?"

"Sometimes it helps to see your situation from another's perspective."

ALEX WAS HANGING OUT on the back porch, watching the parade of people march into the barn when he spotted Cy's truck pulling up behind Jean's sedan. Alex chastised himself. He should have left an hour ago. He had property to look at on the other side of Bear Meadows. His heart sank. He had told Cy the farm's purchase was on hold temporarily, but when Cy asked for details, Alex said nothing. His cousin was becoming understandably impatient. Cy got out of the truck and looked up at the activity at the entrance to the barn.

He turned around, obviously seeking a familiar face. Alex got up and headed for the door, hoping to disappear into the house. But he was too late.

"Hey. Alex, hold up." Alex felt as if he had been shot in the back. He relaxed his shoulders and turned around to face his cousin.

"What the heck is going on?" Cy stood there, arms akimbo. "Why haven't you been returning my calls?"

"I've been busy. We're in negotiations now." He was about to ask Cy how his aunt was when Chance walked out on the porch, followed by the Saint Bernard.

Cy's expression gave a hint of his surprise at seeing the young man. "Hi, Chance."

The younger man slapped his cowboy hat on his head and nodded. "Cy. Long time no see." The two men shook hands.

"I'm surprised to see you. You home for a visit?" Cy asked. Two lines creased the area between his brows.

"I'm home for good. Excuse me, fellas." Chance slapped a hand on Cy's shoulder, clomped down the porch steps and headed up toward the barn.

His brow still furrowed, Cy watched him go. Then he looked at Alex. "He quit, huh?"

Alex shrugged. "He has his reasons."

"What possible—" His words were cut off with the sharp high-pitched cry of a baby. Cy looked through the screen door as if the answer would suddenly appear. His face grew white. "That's not Sera's... No, Sera couldn't have had a baby..." He took off his ball cap and scratched his head. "Could she?"

"Oh, come on, cousin, Sera's skinny as a rail. Did you see a baby bump?"

"I've heard some women get pregnant and don't know they're pregnant." He scratched Rocky behind the ears. Then his hand grew still and he looked up at

Alex with narrowed eyes. "Wait a minute, if Sera was pregnant, it could only be..." His eyes grew dark beneath lowered brows.

Alex held up both hands in self-defense. "Cyrus, how could you even think such a thing?" Even as the words left his mouth, the picture of her lips connecting with his after she wrecked the truck came to mind. And then the goodbye kiss when she left the city. Guilt ate at him. "Besides, that makes no sense."

"Well, then, whose baby? Did she adopt?" When he stopped scratching Rocky behind his ears, the dog wandered down the steps and out of the yard.

"Chance's."

"Chance? Why, he's just a kid."

"Well, I guess not."

"Well, that explains it then."

"What's that?"

"Chance has a baby, brings him or her home and expects Sera to raise the child."

"He's staying and caring for her himself."

"You don't know the boy like I do, Alex. The favored son. Baby of the family. He could do no wrong. He always got away with murder while Sera picked up the slack."

"He's here now."

"Trust me. It won't last."

"Whether he stays or goes, Cy, he and Hope aren't agreeing to the sale."

Cy turned and looked out across the open space between the gate and the barn. In the distance Sera talked with the man wielding the hose from the pressure washer. Cy gave his cousin a look. "I reckon I'll just have to convince Sera to marry me. I told you, cousin. One way or another."

Alex couldn't take his eyes off the subject of discussion. Rocky had arrived. She patted the dog and motioned to the man to follow her. Alex's stomach flipped as if he had eaten a green apple. “What makes you think she’d agree?”

“I’ve known her all my life, Alex. I care for the woman. Her brother is taking advantage of her. Marrying me can help all of us.”

“But you don’t love her.”

Cyrus’s head tilted like Lucky’s when you asked him if he wanted outside. “Why do you care? You’re not pulling a Cyrano de Bergerac on me, are you? I never asked you to court her for me. You do have my back, don’t you?”

Alex gave his country cousin a hard stare when he mentioned the playwright from the 1600s. “What in the world do you know about Cyrano de Bergerac?”

Cy pressed a hand to his chest. “You wound me deeply, my highly educated but seriously clueless cousin. Are you stereotyping me because I’m a simple farmer?”

Alex ran his hand over the stubble on his face. “I’m sorry, you’re right.”

“You better be sorry.” Cy propped one

foot on the step and leaned on it with his elbow. "I saw the movie."

SERA HELPED THE man with the pressure washer find an electric outlet.

Katie motioned to her. "You might want to move the kitties. They're in danger of being pressure washed into space."

Sera followed her gaze. Under the beam stretching across one side of the barn, a kitten dragged its claws along the rough wood and then batted away its sibling. At six weeks old, they were becoming adventurous. "I'll take them downstairs."

She scooped up the kitten who, unlike its tiger-striped mother, was black except for a white patch under its chin. Wriggling to get free, the kitten scratched her wrist and jumped onto the beam.

"Ouch." Sera wiped the blood on her shorts. She felt a tap on her shoulder.

"Need a hand?" Alex gestured at the line of blood on her hand. "I see the kittens are a little feistier than the last time I saw them."

She nodded. "I should've handled them

more, but I've been so busy. They're wild now." She glanced toward the man setting up the pressure washer. He laid out the hose and pointed the wand in their direction. "But if I don't get them downstairs, they're in trouble. The force of the water from that hose will kill them."

"I'll help, but you might want to put on long sleeves." He lunged for a cat, but it jumped out of his way and he landed on the barn floor. He rolled over and rubbed his knee. "I thought I had him."

She laughed. "Tell you what. I'll catch them, you hold them."

"Deal." Grabbing the dusty blanket, Alex pulled the four corners together and held it up for Sera's approval. "Cat hammock."

Sera scooped up the black kitten as it ran up the beam and dropped it into the makeshift hammock. "There's one."

She soon had six kittens in the bag, and together they maneuvered the squirming kittens downstairs and into the space beneath the steps. Sera closed the door leading to the lower level so the kittens weren't able to return to the upper floors, leaving them in darkness. She sank onto the pile of hay. "Whew. That was harder than I expected." She wiped a bead of sweat from her forehead.

Alex sank to his knees next to her and tipped the blanket's contents onto the hay. The kittens scampered out, but as soon as they spied their dozing mother, they settled down to feed. Sera leaned back against the wall.

Alex sat beside her, stretching out his long legs next to hers. "They grow fast, don't they?" He sneezed.

"Bless you. Yes, it's almost time to take them to the shelter. The librarian in town opened up a place. Lucky for me and the kitties. She'll find them homes."

"Are you sure you don't want to keep them?" He sneezed again.

"Bless you again. Are you allergic to cats?"

"I don't know. We never had cats when I was growing up." A kitten, apparently already full, wandered away from its mother and crawled up on Alex's leg.

"I definitely can't keep them. Even more mouths to feed now. I've already got two extra with Chance and Bella."

"Bella. Pretty name. How's that going?"

She didn't answer right away, not wanting to give Alex an even worse impression of her little brother. "Chance is still figuring things out."

He cupped her cheek with one hand and turned so her face was only inches from his. "Don't you think it's time Chance took on some more responsibility around here?"

She lay her hand over his, thinking of their time in the orchard watching the fireworks. Peace and quiet were no more. "He is. He has a baby."

"I mean with the farm. Sera, you've given ten years to this family. When is it your turn?"

Her eyes searched his. "My turn for what?"

His thumb stroked her cheek. He leaned

forward. She thought of the night in the rain, only this time the kiss was his idea.

A shaft of light hit them as the door above opened. "Alex? Sera? You down here?"

At the sound of Cy's voice, Sera pulled back.

Alex's hand slipped from her cheek. The moment was gone, swept away like straw hit with a blast from the pressure washer.

CHAPTER FIFTEEN

"WE'RE UNDER THE STEPS, CY." Sera pulled away and got to her knees. She grabbed a kitten that had already jumped onto the steps, drawn by the light. "Close the door behind you." She was suddenly aware how it must look to Cy. She and Alex alone, in the dark, sitting under the stairs.

Holding the kitten in her arms, she walked over to the lower door and flipped the light switch. Cy eased his big body down the short flight of stairs. When he got to the bottom, he looked from Sera to Alex. "What's going on?"

"I helped her catch the kittens." Alex stood and brushed the hay from his jeans. He smiled at his cousin. "They were in immediate danger."

"Uh-huh." Cy propped his hands on his hips. "Listen, Sera…"

Sera placed the kitten next to the others, and it quickly got into a game with its siblings. "Let's go over to the house."

She opened the lower door and waited for Cy and Alex before shutting it and latching it securely. The two men walked on either side of her. When she looked up, she saw Chance speaking with Kristen. He was leaning against the barn, his cowboy hat tipped back at a rakish angle. Beneath the silver maple, Katie paced back and forth talking on her phone.

"Go on up to the house, Cy. I'll be there in a minute." She left the two men and walked over to her brother, curious what he was discussing with the woman from New York. "What's up?"

Kristen smiled at her as she joined them.

"I was asking Kristen about the best place to put a stage in the barn."

"A stage? Why do we need a stage?

The ceremony is supposed to be under the trellis in the backyard."

"For me. I was thinking after the wedding I could plan a few shows."

"Shows? Singing? You?"

"Well, not just me. I could find people. Local people, or friends passing through on their tours."

"Chance, we're kind of out in the middle of nowhere. Who's going to come to shows in Bear Meadows, Pennsylvania?"

Great, now her little brother thought he was a producer. And how much was this going to cost?

"I've got a problem." Slipping the phone into a pocket of her jeans, Katie walked up the incline to where the three of them stood.

"I'll leave you two alone then." Sera started to leave.

"I'm afraid this concerns you, too, Sera." Katie frowned. "My sister just phoned me. Somewhere in South Dakota, she and Josh have decided to call off the wedding."

Sera felt sick. She was back to two streams of income. She turned and saw Cy and Alex waiting on the back porch. And from the look on Cy's face, if she weren't careful, she would soon be down to one.

ALL ALEX COULD think about was telling his cousin that he, Alex, had his back. That Cy could count on him. So what was he doing taking advantage of the first moment he had alone with Sera to steal a kiss?

Alex recognized both of the women standing with Sera. This had been the first day in a week he hadn't been on the road before breakfast. His stomach dropped as the three women and Chance started toward the house.

"Have a seat, ladies. I'll bring out some iced tea." Sera disappeared into the kitchen.

Brow furrowed, Katie Valentine stopped abruptly in front of him. Then her look of confusion cleared. She reached out her hand. "Alex Kimmel. Fancy meeting you here."

Sera returned with a pitcher and glasses. "You two know each other?"

"Don't forget, Alex has been a New Yorker for years, Sera." Cy leaned against the porch railing, his eyes on Sera.

Alex wondered why his cousin chose to point that out to Sera. Unless he was feeling insecure. Since his announcement about marriage, things had seemed to shift slightly between them. He reached out to shake Katie's hand. "Nice to see you again." He caught Sera's surprised expression.

Sera handed both Katie and Kristen glasses where they had settled onto the swing. "So how do you know each other?"

"We did an interview." Katie looked at Alex. "Do you know Kristen, Alex? She owns Kristen Rose Events."

Alex leaned forward and shook the other woman's hand, relieved that Katie had sidestepped Sera's question. "You handled the wedding for the mayor's daughter last year. I heard you did an exceptional job."

She inclined her head and grinned. "Thank you for saying so."

Chance perched on the porch railing near the swing. "So you think the back corner is the best place for the stage?"

For once, Alex was glad the aspiring country star was self-absorbed. He had no desire to revisit the embarrassing news interview with Katie Valentine.

"Wait a minute, Chance. We have to talk about the wedding." Sera looked at Katie. "So does everything stop?"

Katie gazed up at the porch ceiling, obviously thinking. "I should run this by my parents." She sipped iced tea, her thoughts far away. She paused and said to Sera, "We'll stay on track until my parents come home. In the meantime, let's hope this is just a case of cold feet."

SERA LAY FLAT on her back on the carpet in front of the fireplace, trying to stretch out the pain in her back, caused by the hours of hand weeding the tomato patch. Bella sat in her crib, talking to her in unintelligible baby gibberish.

"How's my girl this morning?" Chance walked into the room and picked up his daughter, who chortled and waved her arms in delight. He looked down at Sera, as if surprised to see her there. "What are you doing on the floor?"

"My back's killing me." Sera brought her knees to her chest. Her back muscles contracted, then relaxed. She sighed with relief.

"Maybe you should go to the chiropractor."

Let's throw some more money away. Sera glanced at her brother, wondering if he could read her thoughts but he was oblivious. He sat in the chair at her feet and shook a rattle for the baby. "I need a check for the carpenter today."

Sera lifted her head from the floor. "What did you say?" She had heard him, but she couldn't possibly have heard correctly. "Why do you want a check from me?"

"The stage in the barn benefits Last Chance Farm, so I figured the farm should pay for the fixing up."

"But neither the wedding nor the farm require a stage. The stage was your idea."

"For possible future concerts."

"Possible? I thought you were making arrangements for singers."

"Well, about that…" He stood, the baby in his arms. "Let me see if Jean's here yet, then we can talk."

Sera dropped her head to the carpet and closed her eyes. Was Chance's lack of maturity her fault? Should she have sheltered him less? Or were a lot of twenty-somethings that immature?

He walked back into the room, his arms free. "Jean's here. She loves looking after Bella." He sat down. "There are a couple things I've been meaning to talk over with you."

Bringing her knees to her chest once again, Sera wrapped her arms around them, then rocked the small of her back on the carpet. Jean was another issue. Why did Chance need a sitter when he wasn't working? Luckily so far Jean had refused payment. "Shoot," she grunted.

"Alex, for one. How long is he staying here?"

Sera gritted her teeth. She wished Chance would drop his assault of Alex. "Until his work's done. Why? He's paying rent and we can use the money."

Chance propped his ankle on his knee and rubbed his whiskered chin. "Did you see his interview with Katie Valentine on TV?"

"How could I? We don't have a television."

Chance tilted his head toward the ten-year-old model on the other side of the room that had been too heavy to carry out. "Yes, you do."

"We don't have cable out here."

"People in the country use satellite dishes."

"I can't afford satellite. I can barely

afford internet. Luckily it comes with the phone line package." She sat up and leaned back on her arms. "So what about Alex?"

"Find the interview online. He doesn't come across as a nice guy. I'm just not sure of his motives. And I don't like how he looks at you."

"What?" Chance had a different girl every day of the week and he didn't like one man in ten years showing an interest in his much older sister? Sera shook her head in confusion.

"I thought you and Cy were an item."

"What made you think that?"

"You went to New York together."

Sera shut her eyes. "It didn't happen. And I don't want to talk about it, Chance. You want me to pay the carpenter. Put the bill on the desk. I have work to do." She pushed herself into a sitting position. "Are we done?"

Staring down at the floor, Chance ran his hand through his wavy locks of hair and took a deep breath. Then he winked and gave her his charming Nashville smile. "I got an offer."

Sera's heart stopped but her brain seemed to speed up, trying to decipher the four simple words. Her words came out hoarse. "You got an offer?"

He nodded and then stood, obviously too excited to sit still. "The Grand Ole Opry needs a backup guitarist." He paced back and forth across the carpet, right over the spot where Sera had just stretched out her back. He turned and held out his hands as if beseeching her. "Do you know where this could lead? Do you have any idea?" His smile was wide as he paced.

"You're going back to Nashville?"

Chance continued his pacing and waving. "Well, heck yeah. Dad would want me to. Don't you?" He paused then and stared at her, still smiling.

"But, Chance, what about Bella?"

Chance shrugged. "She's fine, Sera. I already talked to Jean. She doesn't mind staying a little longer every day. You and Aunt Hope would just have Bella in the evenings, and she sleeps most of the time." He whooped and threw his hands in the air. "Finally, Dad's predictions are coming true."

Sera leaned back against the couch and shut her eyes. Chance would have to celebrate his good news alone, because she just wasn't up for it.

CHAPTER SIXTEEN

UP AT THE crack of dawn, Sera wore a T-shirt and shorts for her morning run. Though the sky in the west was dark, the rising sun was warm and bright. Chance had been gone a week. So far, Jean had been a great help with the baby and showed no signs of tiring. She said she loved being around the baby, especially since Cy showed no signs of marrying.

As the morning went on, the clouds moved in until the only bit of blue was a strip over the far ridgeline. Arms crossed, Sera leaned against the kitchen door watching the storm front approaching from the west. Through the screen she had felt the temperature drop just in the last ten minutes. The ridgetops were already grayed out, and she could see sheets of rain descending across the creek.

"The air coming through that door's getting cold." Wearing her everyday slippers, Aunt Hope padded into the kitchen and came over to stand beside her. She had been much happier since Bella's arrival and the subsequent decision to keep the farm. A rumble of thunder sounded. "Why don't we have soup and sandwiches for lunch?"

"Okay." Sera wasn't hungry, but since Jean had been spending the day with them to care for the baby while Sera was working, they had begun to make a regular meal.

Jean walked in with Bella. The baby's eyes were damp. She lay her head on Jean's shoulder. "The thunder has the baby worked up."

"Lunch will be ready in a bit, Jean." Hope opened the refrigerator door and looked inside.

"I'll make a bottle for Bella."

"I'll get it." Sera found the formula. After a midnight wakening, she had quickly learned how to fix a bottle. "I can't believe how dark it is." Worry ate at her. "Is this supposed to move through quickly?"

Jean sat in the rocker with the fussy baby. "I haven't heard." Taking the bottle, she cradled the baby in her arms. "Is Alex here?"

"He's checking on some property near Shadow Falls." Sera glanced out the window over the sink. "The rain should bring the corn on. I can probably start picking next week."

"Last Friday, the ladies at Vera's asked when your corn would be ready. You should have lots of customers." Hope placed bread and leftover sliced turkey on the table. Thunder crashed somewhere close by, and all three of the women jumped. The bottle forgotten, Bella opened her mouth and wailed.

Sera glanced out the window. "Cy just pulled in."

Jean offered the bottle to the baby, who wanted no part of it. "I told him not to come until dinnertime."

"I wonder what he wants." Cy had been distant since she had told him the sale was off.

He ran out of his truck and up the stairs. The door banged open. He scanned the room, his gaze finally lighting on his mother, rocking the baby. "You have to come with me, Mom."

"What happened?" Jean looked up. "This isn't a good time, Cy. The baby's fussy."

"Too bad. Dad fell down the cellar stairs."

"What?" She looked around as if unsure what to do with the baby. Sera took the child from her arms. "What happened?"

"I guess the stairway was dark, and he was carrying a snack down the stairs and missed a step. Hurry up. He's on his way to the hospital in the ambulance."

"The ambulance?" Her face drained of color, Jean seemed to be in shock.

Sera spotted Jean's purse on the counter

and handed the bag to the woman, who then rushed out the door.

Rocky nudged her knee. "You need to go out, fella? You better hurry up." Sera pushed open the screen door and both dogs brushed past her and ran into the yard and out through the trellis.

Since Jean had left, they didn't bother with soup. After she and her great-aunt ate their sandwiches, Sera picked up her niece and they all went into the den. The room was so dark Sera turned on the desk lamp, then settled onto the couch. Maybe she and Bella would take a nap. The hail pinged on the windows.

"I hope Bob is okay." Settled in the Queen Anne chair with a book, Hope pulled an afghan onto her lap and stared out the window.

"Cy said he'd call." Sera looked down at her niece, whose dark lashes lay like petals on her pink cheeks. Rising carefully from the couch, Sera carried the child to the crib and laid her down. She covered her with Chance's quilt, then returned to the couch with a sigh. "Finally," she said quietly.

The two women sat in silence, the only sound was the occasional rumble of thunder and the whisper of water running down the drainpipe. Sera was almost asleep when her great-aunt spoke.

"I'm surprised your dogs aren't in here. Lucky's afraid of thunderstorms."

Sera's eyes popped open. She was instantly awake. "Oh, no. I let them outside and forgot to bring them back in." She jumped off the couch. "I should find them." Running into the kitchen, she grabbed her poncho off the hook behind the door and sprinted onto the porch.

In the time she, her great-aunt and niece had spent in the den, the temperature must've dropped thirty degrees. Wind and rain whipped sideways, hitting her poncho even while standing under the porch. She started down the steps and almost lost her footing. She looked down. "Oh, no." Pea-sized balls of ice littered the ground and the steps leading up to the porch. She looked west, but there was no sign of the storm easing. "Here, Rocky. Here, Lucky."

Avoiding the ice as much as she could, she eased down the stairs and went hunting for her dogs. Thunder boomed and streaks of lightning followed. She was only a few feet away from the ancient silver maple when a branch came crashing down across the driveway. She dived back toward the house and landed on the gravel. The wet leaves of the long, heavy branch just covered her feet. She got to her hands and knees, her knees stinging from the impact with the gravel. She looked up just in time to see the wind bend the cornstalks sideways. The entire field of green was now no higher than her waist. She stared in disbelief. A light flashed. She turned and looked into headlight beams.

"Sera, what happened?" Cy jumped out of his truck and came and knelt beside her. "Are you hurt?"

"I'm fine. What about your dad?"

"He's fine, too. Mom's with him now. What are you doing outside?"

"I can't find the dogs. They're probably afraid. And the corn. Look at the corn, Cy." She gripped his upper arms and stared up into his face. "The hail and the wind are ruining the corn."

Cy stood and pulled her to her feet as easily as if he were lifting a child. "Don't worry about the corn. Let's look for the dogs."

"I think they're under the mock orange." Sera ran across the lawn and lay down to peer under the bush. Two sets of brown eyes peered out at her. She stretched out her hand. "Come on, fellas. It's okay." But the two dogs just crouched closer to the base of the big bush.

THE STORM STRUCK just as he crossed the bridge over Little Bear Creek. Hail pelted the car. He hoped there was room in the shed so the hail didn't damage Jean's car. Driving around the corner of the house, he was surprised to see Cy's truck, lights on and still running with the driver's-side door open. Then he saw Cy and Sera running across the yard, each leading a wet dog. They disappeared into the house.

Alex parked the car in the shed and then went and pulled Cy's truck next to it. Sera's truck was nowhere to be seen but of the three, he figured Old Blue could handle some hail damage.

He took a deep breath and raced across the open space between the barn and the porch, slipping and sliding on round balls of ice. He opened the screen door just as Sera flew past him. "Sera." He reached for her arm, but she shrugged him off.

Cy stood next to him, just as soaking wet as Sera. "What's she doing?"

"She's checking the corn."

"Why?"

"She has some crazy idea she can save her crop." Cy looked at him, his face grim. "There's no chance in hell." He started down the steps but stopped when Alex grabbed his arm. "What are you doing?"

Cy turned and looked at him. Water streamed down Cy's face, making his curly hair cling to his head. "I'm going to convince Sera the time has come for her to face reality."

Alex watched his cousin take huge strides through the yard. He walked as if the hail were cotton balls instead of ice. Cy reached the arbor and called back to him. "Help Hope dry off those dogs." Then he strode off toward the barn.

Alex looked through the window. Aunt Hope was rubbing off each of the dogs with towels.

Cy still thought he could get away with giving orders. But they were no longer children. Alex headed down the steps and followed his cousin. Sera was in no shape for Cy's strong-arm tactics. For some reason, Alex felt the need to protect her. He walked up the incline and peeked through the open doors of the barn. Empty. The barn had been power washed multiple times in preparation for the wedding. There was neither a cobweb nor a piece of hay to be seen. Round tables and chairs filled the space to the left. But all wedding preparation had been halted. Kristen was back in the city.

Alex was about to go down the small set of stairs to see if Cy and Sera were in the lower part of the barn when something caught the corner of his eye.

He turned. And there they were. Not fifty feet away. Sera was crying, the tears mixing with the rain on her face. Cy stood like a tree, watching her.

"Hold her, man. What's wrong with you?" The words came out of Alex's mouth before he knew what he was saying. But he needn't have worried he would be overheard. His words were drowned out by the thunder of the hailstones pounding the metal roof of the barn. All he could do was stare. But what he saw next felt like one of the hailstones had flown down his throat and spread its iciness through his stomach.

Cy knelt on one knee in the mud at the edge of the cornfield.

"No. No, Cyrus." Alex leaned back against the barn, but he couldn't tear his gaze from the scene in front of him. Cy on bended knee, taking Sera's hand. Sera crying.

He stepped into the barn, out of the icy rain and out of sight of Cy and Sera. And just in time. Sera ran past the barn, followed closely by Cy. Alex tipped his face up to the sky, shivering. *How could Cy ask Sera to marry him, especially when Alex himself was in love with the woman?*

CHAPTER SEVENTEEN

SERA SAT AT the head of the kitchen table, a towel looped around her neck, warming icy fingers by wrapping her hands around the brown mug with the yellow flower. In the air the rich scent of coffee mixed with the heavy odor of wet dog. Lucky and Rocky lay on their beds, each dog with his own beach towel.

"You should take a hot shower." Aunt Hope sat in the rocker, Bella asleep in her arms. "This baby's tuckered out. She'll sleep until you get back."

Sera twisted in her chair, her body felt as if it were weighed down with bricks. "Don't try to carry her, okay?"

"I'll be fine. You go take a hot shower. You'll feel better."

Passing through the hall, Sera stopped

and addressed the eighteen-year-old girl in the graduation picture on the wall. "I doubt it." She stood at the bottom of the carpeted stairs. Never had they looked so steep and so long.

Thirty minutes later she stood in the same spot, still with wet hair but at least shampooed and combed. She tightened the belt around the flannel robe and shuffled down the hall toward the kitchen. Her eighteen-year-old self still smiled. "You don't have a clue," she muttered.

Two empty soup cans sat next to the stove, where Hope stirred a pot. Expecting to see Bella in the high chair and preparing to chastise her great-aunt for lifting the baby, she stopped when she spied Alex in the rocking chair, Bella asleep in his arms.

No one spoke as Sera got bowls from the cupboard. While Hope filled the bowls, Sera took Bella from Alex and carried her into the den, settling her in the crib. The child moved her lips in and out and then sighed softly.

Returning to the kitchen, she sat with Hope and Alex. The only sound was the clinking of spoons against china and the pounding of rain on the roof. Sera scraped the last bit of soup from her bowl. "Has anybody heard from Cy?" At Alex's startled glance she added, "About Bob."

Alex nodded. "He drove back to the hospital. Bob has two cracked ribs and a mild concussion. They're keeping him overnight for observation."

"Thank goodness."

"It could've been much worse." A box of homemade chocolate chip cookies lay on the counter. Taking one for herself, she set the box in the middle of the table. "Where did these come from?"

"Sue Campbell gave them to me. She said you were interested in their house. Where would she get an idea like that?" Hope got up and put the teakettle on the stove.

"I talked to her before Chance came home. I thought her house would be a good location for us. It's only a short distance from Mrs. Hershberger and the church."

"That's true." The teakettle whistled and then quieted as soon as her great-aunt lifted it off the burner. She added the hot water to her cup. "Someone should tell her things have changed. We're not selling."

At her words Sera's shoulders slumped. She looked across the table at Alex. He only shook his head.

It was now or never. "You know, of course, the corn is ruined." Somehow saying the words released the tension in her gut. This was the moment. Letting the air out of the balloon. *Let the air out or break, right?*

Hope brought her cup to the table, dabbing the tea bag up and down, up and down. She reached for a cookie. "Are you sure? A couple days of sun might bring them right back." Her attention was focused on squeezing the tea bag, adding sugar.

Sera winced. No amount of positive

thinking was going to help. "Maybe for the field corn. It still has a month to go. But the sweet corn? I already had orders for next week. It's gone. Ruined."

Hope carried her bowl to the sink and proceeded to run water for dishes. "You have other produce. And the apples."

"The apples are probably on the ground, Hope. Ruined, as well. I have no produce. And if I have no produce, I have nothing to sell and no income. The taxes are past due. It's over."

Hope turned from the sink. For the first time Sera saw her as she truly was. A woman in her nineties. Lines fanned out across her pale cheeks. Her tiny figure was bent. "You're not selling Last Chance Farm."

Tension made her body stiff as Sera stood. "I can't do it anymore, Hope. You and Shawn should be enjoying retirement, relaxing, going on vacations. We just keep plowing the soil, planting, reaping the harvest. Every year it's the same thing. Backbreaking work. And now we lost the harvest." The tightness in her chest was back. She knew she was raising her voice to the older woman but if she didn't, Hope wouldn't hear. "And we never get ahead. Never. The money from the wedding was going to cover the insurance, but now that's gone, too. We're finished." By now she was shrieking at the top of her lungs, something she had never before done. She wondered if perhaps she, too, was finished. A wail came from the den. Aunt Hope started toward the hall.

"Stop. I'll get her." Sera left Alex and her great-aunt in the kitchen and went to soothe the crying baby. She picked up Bella and settled onto the couch, rocking her back and forth. "I'm not sure your father did you any favors bringing you back to Bear Meadows, little girl. You might've been better off in Kentucky."

ALEX STARTED TO follow Sera, but Hope laid a hand on his arm. "Give her a minute. Sit down. I want to talk with you."

Alex took his seat. From the den they heard Sera's murmurs and the occasional protest from Bella. Soon everything was quiet.

"Tea?"

Alex nodded. He sat while the woman prepared his tea and set the cup before him. Then she joined him. "Your cousin wants this farm in the worst way."

"He's just trying to expand, Hope. Can you blame him?"

She stirred her tea, the spoon's clinking against the cup was the only sound in the house. "Did you know my father won this farm in a horse race?"

"Sera mentioned it."

"I wasn't born yet. My parents were married and living in Philadelphia. Remember, this is almost one hundred years ago, just at the end of the First World War. My father fought in Germany, and when he came back he was a little reckless. He would get a job for a while and then get into trouble and lose it.

"My mother told me this story. I was

her firstborn. A little bit like Sera, I took responsibility for everyone and everything.

"Divorce wasn't common in those days, of course, but my mother wasn't about to have a family with a man who couldn't keep a job and gambled away anything he did make. She threatened to go back home. To leave him.

"My father loved her. More than anything. And more than gambling. He had nothing. So he took one last gamble. He bet ten years of labor working in a factory against a small farm in the Allegheny foothills, sight unseen. He knew if he lost this bet, he lost my mother, too. But his horse won.

"So they took the train to Bear Meadows, not knowing what they were getting into. On the way there my mother told my father this was his last chance. That if he gambled again she was gone, back to Philadelphia. And he never did. Once I was born, he started raising racehorses, although he never again bet on a single race.

"This is why it's so important to keep this farm in the family. The Callahan family. This is our last chance. If Chance stays in Nashville and Sera goes to New York, they won't have anyplace to come home to."

Alex thought of his dream. *This is your last chance, son.*

Was the dream a warning about the evicted couple back east? He had found a nursing home the husband and wife could both be in and had put the couple on a waiting list. But maybe the dream was about finding out whether or not he had a home.

CHAPTER EIGHTEEN

"So, now what?" Alex picked up a stick and tossed it ahead in the lane. Lucky raced after it.

"I have nothing to sell and therefore no income." Sera reached down and ruffled the fur of the animated dog walking between them. "You and Rocky have come to terms, eh?"

Alex gave her a sideways glance that generated goose bumps. "Big, mean dog, eh?"

She laughed. "I couldn't help giving you a hard time that night. You were so arrogant."

"Me? Arrogant?" He slapped his hand to his chest in disbelief.

She reflected on all that had happened since the night she gave Alex a ride. "It feels strange not to have anything to do."

"I never realized how much weather affects a farmer's livelihood."

"Everything. The corn, tomatoes, peppers. Everything was beaten to a pulp last week." When they reached the top of the hill and the apple orchard, Sera was not surprised. The ground was littered with apples. "Apples, too. It just wasn't meant to be, Alex."

"So what are you going to do?"

"Sell to your cousin. What choice do I have?" When Alex didn't answer, she tore her gaze from the shredded leaves of the apple trees to Alex's thoughtful face. "Well?"

He finally looked at her. "You could marry him."

A jolt went through her at his suggestion. "What good would that do? Chance still owns half."

"I don't think it would take much to persuade Chance to stay in Nashville. Aunt Hope would get the Century Farm designation like she wanted." He avoided her gaze, instead looking across the creek at Cy's

American flag whipping in the breeze. "After all, he did ask you, didn't he?"

Shock tore through her system. "How do you know about that? Did he tell you?"

Alex shook his head. "I was spying. During the storm. I saw him get down on one knee and I kind of figured that's what was going on."

Laughing, Sera relaxed. "There's a proposal for the record books. In the middle of a hailstorm." Kicking apples aside, she continued strolling through the orchard.

"I gather you didn't give him an answer." Alex followed a step behind.

"No, I didn't. Really, Alex, how could I accept? We don't love each other. What kind of marriage would it be?"

Alex shrugged. "I suppose you know the story of Last Chance Farm?"

The reminder caused her heart to twist. "I do. But it can't be helped. Even if I were willing to marry him for the sake of keeping the farm in the family, how could that be fair to Cy? Besides, I think he likes Dr. Hannah."

"He likes you, too."

They stopped at the crest of the hill. Down below, the log cabin sat quietly next to the other orchard, the one with the apples that were of no use. "I'm not sure Cy is capable of love, except for his business. Every move he makes always comes back to how it impacts the farm."

"What about those apples?" Alex pointed to the orchard Sera's mother had planted ten years earlier. "They have to be good for something."

Sera stopped thinking about marrying Cy and followed his line of sight. "They were protected from the wind. They're still on the trees. Figures. But I told you. They're not good eating apples." Sera marveled at the crop below. Too bad. So why did her mother plant them if they weren't good for anything?

ALEX SAT AT the rolltop desk. Cy and Sera occupied the two wing chairs. Despondent at the recent turn of events, Hope was nowhere to be seen. The piles of paper on the desk had been replaced with a neat stack of folders. Busy making contacts in Nashville, Chance had agreed to the sale. He was talking about taking Bella south.

"I compared the sale of other properties in the area, and this is the figure I came up with." Alex wrote the number on a piece of paper and placed it in the middle of the desk so both parties could see the sum.

Cy coughed and cleared his throat. "Are you kidding?"

"Comparable properties." Alex leaned back in the chair and waited for his cousin to digest the number which, as far as he was concerned, was fair to both parties.

His heart ached when he saw the sadness in Sera's eyes. The number could have been in the millions and the look would've been the same. "If you need a moment…"

Alex looked up at the sound of a knock. Shawn stood in the doorway.

Sera paused and turned around. "Shawn,

do you need something? We're kind of busy right now."

"I'm here to stop you from doing something you'll regret, Sera." Green cap in hand, the slight man stepped farther into the room.

Alex's chest seized when he saw who stood behind Shawn.

"Hello, son." Max Kimmel followed Shawn into the den.

"Dad, what's going on?"

Taking Shawn by the elbow, the two men approached the desk. "It seems the document search on the property wasn't complete."

Alex bristled. Leave it to his father to question his abilities. But Alex knew the law. "The title search was done properly. I did it myself. I went through the deeds here at the farm and at the courthouse."

"Oh, I'm not talking about deeds, son. Mind if we sit down?"

"Have a seat on the couch." Hope entered the room. Alex looked from Hope to his father to Shawn and wondered what the three were up to. There was no doubt Hope and Shawn didn't want the farm sold. "Sera has Chance's power of attorney. Hope signed over her share to the kids when Sera's parents died. There's nothing more to be done, Dad."

"Oh, but there is. Hope, care to explain?"

Hope sat between the two men on the couch and, her eyes on Sera, squared her shoulders. "Your grandfather, my brother and the original Chance, knew that the Callahan men had a propensity for gambling, Sera. He didn't want to take any chances on the farm being lost to the family. When the farm was left to the two of us, we promised our mother the farm would never leave the family."

"Aunt Hope, please, we've been over this. That was a hundred years ago. Times change." Sera ran her hands through her hair.

"When Shawn showed up here looking for work after his tour in Vietnam, he and your grandfather became friends." Hope placed a hand on Shawn's shoulder. "But they were more than friends, Sera. Your grandfather Chance was Shawn's uncle."

Sera couldn't believe what she was hearing. Two red spots colored Aunt Hope's pale cheeks, and one corner of her mouth drooped. For a minute Sera feared the woman was having a stroke. As she watched, her great-aunt and the man who had lived on the farm ever since she could remember shared a glance. And that's when she saw it. "You have the same eyes."

Hope nodded and sighed. Her shoulders relaxed, as if a weight had been lifted from them. "Shawn is my son, Sera. His father and I were planning to be married when Pearl Harbor was bombed. We didn't think he would be gone long, so we postponed the wedding. Only Seamus Campbell didn't come back. If he had, we would've married and Shawn—" She twisted the tiny emerald ring on her finger. Shawn reached for her hand.

Sera met Shawn's gaze. "You're my—"

"First cousin once removed." His eyes

twinkled and for the first time Sera recognized her father's twinkle.

"When I found out I was pregnant, I went to Georgia and stayed with friends of the family, the Murphys. Back in those days, having a baby out of wedlock was just not done. I didn't want to bring shame on the family. I thought Seamus would be back before I showed. Then we found out he had been killed in action. I had no choice. I was twenty. The Murphys adopted Shawn and raised him as their own."

"How did he end up here?"

Shawn explained. "My parents told me the truth when I was a child. After I came back from 'nam, I hitchhiked north. I wanted to see my home. And I never left."

She took a breath yet her lungs felt empty, as if a weight sat on her chest. She tried again but still couldn't get air.

Asleep upstairs, Bella chose that moment to let out a lusty cry. Still taking care of her husband, Jean hadn't yet returned to babysitting. As Sera rose to respond to the crying child, she was brought full circle to the present. The reason they were all in the room. "Be right back."

When she returned to the den, the baby happy in her arms, no one had moved. She settled the baby in her great-aunt's lap and returned to her chair. "Where were we?"

"Sera, you can't continue. What about Bella? This is her home."

"Don't you understand? I can't take care of all of you—you, Hope, and you, Shawn, and the baby—and run a business. And despite Shawn being your son, you signed off, remember? Dad left his share to us."

"So Shawn and I go to a home and Bella gets adopted."

"Bella is Chance's child, Hope. It's his decision. And you're not going to a home. The Hunters are selling their house, which isn't far from Mrs. Hershberger's. After we pay our bills, we'll have enough for a down payment. You'll be closer to your friends. You won't be stuck out here in the country all by yourself. It's not good, Aunt Hope. You need socialization."

"So do you, Sera."

"My offer's still on the table, Sera." Cy gave her a look.

She pressed her fingers to her eyes. "Let's get this over with, Alex."

"Just a minute. Shawn is more than a long-lost relative." Max Kimmel stood, set his briefcase on the end table and opened the clasp. Pulling out an envelope, he glanced sharply at his son. "We can't be throwing elderly people out of their home again, can we, son?"

Alex's face reddened.

"You can't sell Last Chance Farm, Sera." Max pulled a crisp manila envelope from the briefcase and opened the flap. He peered in and carefully withdrew a yellowed sheet of lined paper. "You can't sell Last Chance Farm, Sera, because you don't own the property free and clear." He laid the paper on the table in front of Sera.

"Sure I do. Aunt Hope signed off when

we transferred the deed after my parents died. Chance and I own the farm. Free and clear."

Max tucked his chin as if pondering her words. "Why don't I read you this document? The ink is a bit faded." He picked up the paper.

"I, Chance A. Callahan, do hereby transfer my ownership of Last Chance Farm to Shawn Murphy, as payment for debt incurred in a poker game on this day, the thirteenth of October, 1969."

Max returned the paper carefully to the middle of the table. "So you see, Miss Callahan, the farm did not legally pass from your grandfather to your father because your grandfather didn't own the property at the time of his death. Hope's share belongs to you and your brother. But the share your father left you was invalid. Shawn shares equally in the ownership of this property. You cannot sell to Cyrus Carter."

CHAPTER NINETEEN

WHEN SHE RETURNED from her morning run, Alex's well-traveled black leather carry-on sat by the kitchen door. Her heart skipped a beat. She heard his feet pounding down the stairs. A minute later he came from the hallway into the kitchen.

She turned her back just in time on the pretense of getting a cup of coffee.

"I was hoping I'd see you before I left."

"Cup of coffee?" She waited, her back still toward him. Every sense in her body seemed to be tuned to his presence in the room.

"Sure."

She grabbed an extra cup and poured the coffee. The room seemed to be getting smaller. Pasting a bright smile on her face, she turned and handed him the cup. "Why don't we sit out on the porch?" The kitchen was definitely too small. Rocky and Lucky followed them out the door.

Avoiding the swing on the far side, Sera sat in one of the rocking chairs. Alex took the other and propped his feet on the porch railing. "I'm going to miss this." He sipped his coffee and then sighed deep. Rocky settled between the two chairs. Alex let his hand drop down to scratch the big dog behind the ears. "I'll miss Cujo, too."

Sera smiled into her cup. "Once you're back in the city you'll forget all about us."

"Hardly."

She shivered.

"I'm sorry my father disrupted your plans." Alex rocked slowly back and forth. "You have no idea how sorry."

"You could've knocked me over with a feather when your dad read from that wrinkled piece of paper."

"I can't believe your grandfather would bet the farm in a poker game."

"A high-stakes poker game. Like Aunt Hope always said, the men in this family are gamblers. If Shawn hadn't stepped in and won, we wouldn't be living here."

"Yet he never said anything. Just let things go on as usual."

"Shawn didn't want to take the chance of exposing his mother's secret and embarrassing her. But now everybody's happy. Hope will see Last Chance Farm get awarded Century Farm designation from the Commonwealth of Pennsylvania. Shawn is recognized as a Callahan. Thanks to all the money he saved over the years he was able to pay the taxes and the insurance. And my dear little brother gets to have his cake and eat it, too." She wondered if Alex heard the bitterness in her voice.

"What a story." Alex leaned forward and set his cup on the railing. "I should go."

Sera looked down and bit her lip. The time had come. She felt Alex pass by, thinking he was going to fetch his bag, but he stopped in front of her. Gently he took the cup from her hands, placed it next to his and then pulled her from the rocker. She faced him.

"Sera, come to New York with me."

Despite the pain in her chest, she laughed. "Money may not be an issue anymore, Alex, but Aunt Hope is still in her nineties, Shawn in his seventies and there's a baby in the house."

"The baby isn't yours."

"The baby is my niece. I have a responsibility to her."

"Sera, I'm going to ask you one more time. Come to New York with me."

She stared into pleading brown eyes, committing to memory the color, the laugh lines at the corners, the dimple in his left cheek when he smiled, and the way one lock of hair would flop onto his forehead when the wind blew. "Spending time with you this summer has meant so much to me, Alex, but—"

"You're afraid to take the gamble. That's what's really going on, isn't it?"

Alex cupped her face with his hands. "You don't have to stay anymore, Sera. You can finish what you started. Go back to school. Resume the career you wanted ten years ago. Get to know the city again…with me."

She lay her head on his chest, shut her eyes and listened to the beating of his heart. He wrapped his arms around her and held tightly. He was right, of course. She couldn't risk leaving everything she knew for the unknown. He began to kiss her, it was a long, slow kiss. When he pulled back, she said, "You kissed me that time."

His smile was sad. "I did, didn't I?"

He picked up his bag, walked down the steps and out to his car. Then he drove away without looking back, and for that she was grateful.

She went in the kitchen, refilled her cup and opted for the porch. There was little to do. The corn had been destroyed, most of the tomatoes and flowers were gone, so she just sat and rocked. Shawn would pay the fall taxes.

She didn't know how much time had passed when she heard car tires on gravel. Her heart skipped a beat at the thought that Alex had returned. Would he insist she go with him? She smiled. What would she do if he did? She was entertaining the thought of how to answer him when the familiar black SUV pulled up to the gate. But Alex wasn't in the driver's seat. She stood and walked over to see who it was.

"Sera, you'll never guess." Katie jumped out from behind the wheel at the same time her mother emerged from the passenger seat.

"The wedding's back on." Babs waved her arms in the air as she came around the front of the vehicle. "Isn't that wonderful? We're having a barn wedding after all."

CHAPTER TWENTY

"SO, HOW'S BELLA?" Chance Callahan swung his guitar over his shoulder and picked up his satchel.

"She's growing like a weed. She has four teeth, Chance."

"She only had two when I left. What about Shawn and Hope? You could've knocked me over with a feather when you told me what happened. How are they handling things?"

With a wave at Scooby, busy renting out a car at his kiosk, Sera chuckled. "Pure chaos. Hope took Cousin Shawn to her quilt party with the church ladies and introduced him as her son."

"You're kidding."

"She wanted to take Bella, but I

wouldn't let her. She's too heavy for Hope to carry."

Chance's brow wrinkled. "She's a baby."

"She's a growing baby, Chance." Leaving the airport lobby, Sera held the door for her brother, guitar case in one hand and duffel bag in the other.

The parking lot wasn't full. Sera had found a spot in the first row next to a late-model sports car.

"Let's take that one." Chance tilted his head toward the shiny silver vehicle as he opened his door.

Sera tugged open the door of the truck. "Don't I wish?" She turned the key and for a minute she thought the engine would catch first try, but it ground to a halt. She looked at her brother. "I need a battery." The engine caught on a second try. She paid for parking and pulled out onto the road.

Chance took off his hat and laid it crown up between them. "Alex still around?"

She put on her turn signal, looked left,

then right. "No. He did what he needed to." She didn't say how much she missed him, talking to him, having him around.

"Did you watch that interview online like I asked you to?"

"I haven't had time." Plus she didn't really want to see how Alex had come across to others. "And it doesn't matter anymore."

When they arrived at the back gate of their house, Sera shut off the engine. "What do you think?"

Chance got out of the truck and looked around in awe. "This place looks amazing."

She followed his gaze. The out-of-control shrubs around the base of the barn had been trimmed or removed. Mulch lined the foundation as did pots of sunflowers and zinnias. "The Valentines hired a landscaper. Can you believe the difference?"

Chance propped one arm on the hood of the truck and finally met her gaze. "So let's see if I have this straight now. We're not selling."

"You and I only own half the farm, the half Hope signed over to us. Shawn owns the other half."

"And he won't agree to sell."

"Apparently he's saved every penny he's ever earned so paying bills isn't a problem at the moment. Although we shouldn't drain his savings. The farm should still sustain itself somehow."

Chance plopped his hat on his head and crossed his arms, looking at the farm as if he had never seen it before. "Maybe I should stay, Sera. Maybe it's time for you to go out into the world."

"You're making me dizzy, bro. One minute you're staying, the next you're going." But a flash of excitement shot through her. She thought of Alex's request to go to the city with him. Could it be? Could it happen? But the flash was gone as quickly as it had begun, like fireworks in the night. Maybe he actually thought he could live here, but she knew she couldn't count on him. "Is there a reason you're thinking of staying?"

He shrugged and then bounced up the porch steps and disappeared into the kitchen.

When Sera entered the kitchen, Chance was inspecting the inside of the refrigerator. "Finally, you guys have some food."

"Don't even think about it. It's all for the wedding."

"Come on. They won't miss one bite." But he only withdrew the iced tea pitcher. Looking in the upper cupboard, he found a bag of chips. "Is Alex coming to the wedding tomorrow?"

"I don't know." Sera settled in the rocking chair.

"You need to know what kind of man he is."

"I already know."

"You're looking through rose-colored glasses, sis. He throws old people out of their houses."

She laughed. "He does not."

"A couple years ago his company was putting in one of those theater shopping mall complexes down east. One old couple refused to sell. They wanted to stay in their home for the rest of their days. Sound familiar?"

She got a queasy feeling in her stomach. "It wasn't his idea."

"He was interviewed by Katie Valentine. He basically admitted to using eminent domain to evict them from their house, so his company could build their mall. As if that wasn't bad enough, the home they went to couldn't accommodate the husband, so they went to two different nursing homes." He took a big bite. "All thanks to your new friend."

"I know all about this, Chance."

"Well, he didn't appear to be such a great guy in the interview. The story went national."

Alex's explanation of what happened and the interview sounded like two different stories. No wonder Alex's father was upset with his son. She rocked back and forth.

WITH HER MANY CONNECTIONS, Carrie had finagled an invitation to the wedding.

When Alex refused to go, she asked Will to be her plus one. Since she was driving, Alex suggested they overnight at his parents' home, knowing his mother would love the company. Although he wasn't going to the wedding, after leaving on bad terms the last time, he was coming to town, hoping to make amends with his mom. It was time to clear the air with his father, too.

After an uneventful drive, they arrived at his parents' place. As his friends grabbed their suitcases, he went in the house and stood in the entry. Everything was quiet. "Mom?"

"Up here, honey."

He bounded up the stairs. His mother fluffed a sheet over the bed in the guest room. "Straighten that out, would you? I'm getting this room ready for Carrie. She and Will are with you, aren't they?"

"They're downstairs." He pulled the wrinkles out of the sheet. "Listen, I'm sorry about the last time I was here."

"You need to fix things with your father."

"I know."

"And who knows, maybe in a few years you'll want to come back to the area." She smiled.

"I doubt he'll ever forgive me for taking the job in New York after graduation."

"Maybe the wedding will provide neutral ground. I'm excited to go tomorrow. Aren't you?"

"I'm not going."

She straightened. "Why not? Your friends are going."

He helped her tuck the corners of the sheet and cover the bed with the handmade quilt. "I'm not invited," he lied.

"It's a barn wedding. One more won't make a difference." She fluffed the pillows and tossed them against the headboard. "Besides, don't you want to see Sera?"

CHAPTER TWENTY-ONE

EVEN DURING THE DAY, the fairy-tale lights lent an air of mystery to the upper reaches of the old barn.

Sera wore the dress borrowed from Katie Valentine, a light blue-green sleeveless number with a long flowing skirt. As she ran her hand along the soft material, Sera felt like a princess.

Just a few weeks ago she thought she was out of options. Now possibilities were coming out of the woodwork. Was Kristen Rose right? Could she make money from the farm? When farming involved making hay and growing corn, or raising cattle like Cy, the odds were good she wouldn't succeed. But events? Along with certified organic produce? That took planning. That she could do.

Cyrus Carter had proposed, and she actually might have considered marriage if Chance hadn't appeared when he did. But now things were looking completely different. Shawn prevented her from selling, but her brother had given her an idea.

Chance was home. She had four streams of income and a reinstated scholarship offer. Cy had told her to take her time making up her mind, but she didn't need any time. No to the marriage proposal and no to selling him the farm. At any price.

She shook off the thoughts for another time. The day of the wedding had arrived. Wendy, her mother, Babs, and maid of honor, Katie, were upstairs in Sera's bedroom. Josh, his father, Brad, and Matt, the best man, were in the den. And Holly, Suzanna Campbell and Shelly, a recent graduate of a pastry school, were in the kitchen, preparing the hors d'oeuvres for the cocktail party before the reception.

The tables had been covered with white tablecloths and set up throughout the barn. Sera walked over to make sure the holes in the floor had been covered. She grimaced as she pictured guests falling through the floor. Definitely bad publicity for her first event. But the holes were firmly covered.

Mason jars filled with fall flowers and tiny votive candles decorated the tables. Chance's guitar already waited for him on the corner stage. After the wedding, the guests would enjoy cocktails on the lawn while the caterers prepared the buffet.

She checked her watch, noting the time had come. The sun set in the west, a flowing ribbon of orange and pink across the far ridgeline, like a line of summer lipstick. Standing in the barn opening, her heart swelled with pride at the sight of the guests seated on benches between the barn and the arbor. Josh and Matt, a cowboy from Montana, stood next to the rose-covered trellis.

Sera decided to stay right where she was, the better to see the bride when she emerged from the kitchen. She was so engrossed in watching the back door that she didn't pay attention to the figure coming toward her. "Sera." Alex stood before her in a familiar gray suit, white shirt and apricot tie. "You look lovely."

"So do you." Her heart skipped a beat. "I didn't think you were coming."

"My mom talked me into it." He motioned toward the house. "Here they come."

The sight of the bridesmaid took Sera's breath away. Launa Starr was a weather forecaster who had worked with Wendy in Miami. Dark, curly hair fell down her back, contrasting with the simple salmon pink gown. Katie followed, equally arresting in a dress of the same color, but in a different style. When Chief McAndrews's seven-year-old daughter, Riley, emerged in a white dress with a pink bow, tossing rose petals on the runner, the crowd murmured in appreciation. Her smile was wide. Her fine blond hair was piled on top of her head with pink ribbons.

There was a collective gasp when Wendy

appeared. She wore a slim satin dress. Her dark hair swept her face in a smooth line.

From where they stood, Sera couldn't hear the vows, but when Alex took her hand she pulled away. "They'll need my help with the cocktail party when the ceremony is over." And without looking at the man next to her, she made her way toward the house. Under the arbor, the groom took his bride in his arms and kissed her with such passion, Sera had to look away. Love was such a complicated emotion.

The wedding party moved to the silver maple for pictures, and the bartender quickly became busy.

Sera smiled at the sight of Aunt Hope sitting in a rocking chair on the porch, a flute of champagne in her hand and a plate of cheese squares and grapes nearby. "You look comfortable."

"Imagine, Sera. A wedding at our farm."

Sera nodded. "Kristen Rose is a miracle worker. When Wendy first asked me if she could use the barn for her wedding,

I thought she was kidding." She settled into the empty rocker next to her great-aunt. "The barn looks great."

"I was still thinking I could do some shows." Chance pushed through the screen door and sat on the steps. "There is a lot of local talent around. What do you think?"

Another income stream. "All we can do is try."

THEY WERE EATING lemon chicken and parsley potatoes when Max asked Alex a direct question. "Throw anybody out lately?"

"Don't start, Max." Beverly placed her hand on his.

"What are you talking about?" When nobody answered, Carrie directed her question at Alex. "What is he talking about?"

"Nothing." For a minute the table was silent.

When he avoided looking at her, Carrie shook Alex's shoulder. "You didn't tell your parents?"

Alex shrugged.

"Alex, it's one thing to take a bullet for the company, but you should've explained to your parents."

"It doesn't matter, Carrie."

"Yes, it does." She looked across the table. "Mr. Kimmel, the eminent domain case wasn't Alex's. The case was initiated by my father."

Max threw her a shrewd look. "Alex was interviewed on television. By Katie Valentine, in fact. Looked pretty clear to me."

"They assumed the case was his because he was handling the transaction, however, the decision to use eminent domain was my father's and that of the company that had hired us. When the reporter started asking Alex questions, he didn't say anything to dispel the assumption. Your son was loyal to the company, Mr. Kimmel."

"Why didn't you tell us?" his mother asked.

Alex shrugged again.

His father looked at Carrie, one bushy eyebrow raised. "Your father allowed it to happen?"

"Dad felt terrible, but we figured a story in a small community would be dead the next day. By the time the story went national, it was too late for something like a press release." She looked at her friend. "Alex told him not to worry about it."

"I always knew you'd be great at the law. But I worried about your ethics."

"His ethics are top-notch, Mr. Kimmel," Carrie said.

Uncomfortable at being the center of attention, Alex stood. "I'm getting a drink. Anyone want anything?"

"I should have known better. I owe you an apology," Max said, rising. Alex pressed him to sit.

"It's fine, Dad. I understand."

"Well, if that's the case, then how about

grabbing one of those chocolate cupcakes for me?" Max smiled at him, obviously relieved the fiasco hadn't been his son's doing.

"Mom said to watch your sugar intake," Alex half teased. But his mother looked so relieved at the turn of events he doubted she cared about a cupcake.

"That's what I'm doing. I'm watching myself eat a cupcake."

CHANCE HAD FOUND a local guitar player and fiddle player. The sounds of their warming up wafted across the night air. Light from the rising moon shone above the distant ridgetops. The crowd was scattered, waiting for the moon's appearance. Wendy and Josh posed, kissing every few minutes, waiting for the photographer to get the perfect picture with the moon in the background. Sera had a feeling they didn't mind waiting. This moment would last long in their memories. And Last Chance Farm had been a significant part.

Matching the color of the bridesmaids'

dresses, the moon rose like a big tangerine. Sera heard her brother on the microphone calling everyone inside. Sera stood alone, looking at the moon.

"You pulled it off."

She didn't need to turn. She'd recognize that voice anywhere. When Alex put his arms around her, she just leaned back into him. "I didn't. Kristen Rose Events did. I just provided the setting." She focused again on the moon, which seemed to get smaller as it rose in the sky.

"Well, it works." He nodded at the moon. "Who else could pull that off?"

"I was surprised to see you here."

"My dad helped Josh out of a jam a couple years ago, so he and my mother were invited. I think I'm what you might call a wedding crasher."

"I've heard about guys like you."

With a slight smile, he narrowed his eyes. "I was only following Mom's orders."

She tilted her head. "You seem happy."

"My father and I have a temporary détente. Thanks to Carrie."

"I'm happy for you."

"The last time I was here, Shawn and Hope made their fateful announcement. Anything else new?"

"My brother's home. He's discovered he's traveling a different path, too, quite by accident. But no, he's decided to live here and raise his child."

"And what are you doing?"

She turned and faced him. "I don't know..."

"If Chance is here..."

"Chance's plans are as changeable as the weather, Alex." Suddenly, she realized she had fallen in love with the man before her, but at the same time knew her feelings didn't matter in the greater scheme of things. She placed her palms on either side of his face. "You know the only thing we do have in common is we both have first names with four syllables."

"That's just silly. We have plenty of things in common. We both like hard apple cider, for instance. Please come with me, Sera. This is your chance at a new life." He leaned forward and pressed his lips to hers.

"What do you think you're doing?"

Sera was so caught up in kissing Alex in the bright light of the full moon she heard the words, but dismissed them. She figured, hoped, someone else would handle the problem.

She wrapped her arms tighter around Alex's neck, wanting their kiss to go on forever.

But Alex pulled away. When she opened her eyes, she then realized he didn't pull away as much as was pulled away.

"Cyrus?" She looked into her neighbor's red face, whose gaze was fixed on his cousin.

Cy Carter stood with clenched fists, scowling at them both. "I should have known."

"Cy, don't get excited. We didn't plan this." Alex held up both hands.

"Sure you did. New York lawyer. I

should have known. I turn my back for one minute and you swoop in." His fist connected with Alex's jaw.

Sera's heart leaped into her throat. "Cy, what are you doing?" She tried to stop his advance on Alex lying in the grass. But trying to stop Cy was like trying to stop an angry bull. Cy had one thing on his mind. Total destruction of his cousin.

"So you're the reason she said no. You've been moving in on her since I brought you here."

"You didn't bring me here, Cyrus. If you recall, you left me stranded." Alex wiped a trickle of blood from his lip with the back of his hand.

"Don't give me that lawyer speak. You were supposed to talk her into selling, you rat."

Alex held up one hand. "Cy, stop."

"Why not just marry her, you said. And here you are, kissing her, right under my nose."

On her knees beside Alex, Sera looked

from one man to the other. “You told him he should marry me?”

“It’s not like that, Sera.”

“Did you, or didn’t you?”

“Well, I may have said those words, but I didn’t really mean them.”

She rose slowly and lifted her gaze to the moon. Behind her, Chance’s voice grew louder on the clear night air. She looked toward the barn. Between all the dancers, she could see her little brother, playing her father’s guitar, black hair flopped over one eye, and his rich tenor drawing in his audience.

Who did she think she was kidding? She wasn’t going anywhere. Chance was. Nothing had changed.

CHAPTER TWENTY-TWO

THE THREE MEN sat on the open tailgate of Cy's new truck listening to Chance Callahan sing a country Western song. Light spilled from the open doorway of the big barn, but Cy's truck was parked next to the mock orange bush, out of sight of the guests.

"How's your jaw?" Cy leaned an arm on the side of the truck and looked at the moon.

Perched on the opposite side of the tailgate, Alex emptied what was left of the ice on the gravel and wrung out the towel. He scooped a handful of ice from the cooler in the bed of the truck and reapplied the compress to his jaw. "Can't feel a thing." He glanced at his father sitting between the two men. "What happened to your tie?"

Max shrugged. "It got smeared with cupcake icing somehow, so I took it off." The song ended and the fiddle player began a solo.

Alex returned his gaze to the still brightly lit barn. "Nice party."

"Yep." Cy handed him a beer from the cooler behind him. "That city gal did a nice job."

"Have a beer for me? My throat's kind of dry." Chance appeared from behind the shrub.

Cy grabbed another beer from the cooler and tossed it to him. "Nice job tonight."

"Thanks." Chance pushed his hat back and took a long drink.

Alex braced himself for another assault.

"I happened to overhear your friend Carrie."

Alex struggled to think what Chance might be talking about. Carrie had been talking to everyone all evening. "About what in particular?"

"About that thing on Katie's news show when it looked like you threw old people out of their house. That thing your dad is always talking about."

"Oh, please, don't bring that up again. Bev is never going to let me live that down." Max rubbed a hand across his forehead.

Alex chuckled. "Hate to be wrong, huh, Dad?" He elbowed him in the side. His father chuckled in return.

"Anyway, it appears I was mistaken about your character." Taking another swig, Chance continued to focus on the barn.

Alex gave him a hard stare. Maybe the boy was finally becoming a man. "I was only trying to do right by your sister, who, in case you don't realize, works her butt off for this place."

"Yeah, yeah, I know." Chance scuffed the ground with the toe of his boot.

"I wanted to tell you I came across a notebook of your mother's about those apple trees she planted up by Shawn's cabin."

Chance twisted his body until he could look Alex fully in the face. "What about them?"

"You have to read her notes, but she planted cider apples. That's the project your dad borrowed for. The cost projections are all in your mom's notebook."

"Really?" Chance pursed his lips, exactly as Alex saw Sera do dozens of times when she was mulling something over. "Go on."

"Mike at the airport bar is making his own brand of hard cider. You might want to reach out to him, see if he's interested in your apples."

"Hmm. Another income stream."

Alex nodded. "Another income stream."

"So if I do that, and keep up with the work around here, are you going to rescue her from all this?"

"Sera doesn't need to be rescued by anyone. She needs to save herself. Did she tell you her scholarship was renewed?"

Chance's head jerked up so quickly his hat fell off. "What? No! When did that happen?"

"A few weeks ago." From the changing expressions on the young man's face, Alex was certain Sera had failed to share that bit of news with her brother.

Chance lifted the bottle high in the air as if he were toasting the bride and groom. "Well, then, she has to go."

"She won't leave."

Chance picked up his hat and placed it firmly on his head. "Maybe it depends on you. I better get back to work." He strolled off toward the barn.

"Hey, wait up." Max jumped off the tailgate. "I want to check out the rest of the cupcakes."

Cy gave Alex a look. "Maybe that boy's finally becoming a man."

Alex watched his father and the singer head for the barn, where the twinkling lights turned the evening into a celebration. If he was right, if Chance was finally growing up, then maybe now Sera would be able to let go of the past and look toward the future. A future that he hoped included him.

SERA SAT AT a corner table, a glass of white wine in her hand. Though she still wore the pretty dress borrowed from Katie, she no longer felt like a princess. Like Cinderella, she was resigned to the ashes, or in her case, the garden.

"I need to talk with you."

She didn't bother to look over her shoulder. "Your assignment is over. You failed."

Alex reached for her hand and pulled her across the crowded dance floor and outside, where the harvest moon rose high in the sky. He looked down at the woman in his arms. "I haven't failed yet."

She stepped back, but he tightened his hold. "Your cousin isn't getting this farm. Why you suggested he propose..."

"I admit I said those words." He waited until she looked up at him, then brought his face close to hers. "At first I'd just been talking off the top of my head. But it was wrong, stupid of me." He took a deep breath. "Especially once I realized a few things. A few really important things… about us."

When she rested her head on his shoulder, he pulled her closer, grateful for what they had. She needed time to process, and he would give her time. One dance, two dances. But Monday morning he would have to be back in New York. His project here was finished, and he had no reason to return. They turned in slow circles, as Chance crooned a sultry ballad.

The drama of the evening dissipated as they danced under the light of the harvest moon. Over her head, Alex took in the green fields stretching up to the orchard on the hill, the big white barn, the old homestead, and marveled that Sera had kept the place going as long as she had. Cy was right. Sera was a strong woman. He just hoped she would finally realize the time had come for a change. He followed her gaze to the lights in the barn.

"He's great, isn't he?" she asked.

They continued to move to the sultry music. "He's talented, no doubt."

She looked up at him. "Then how can I ask him to give up his dream?"

The blissful sensation of being in the moment faded, as Alex digested her question. He swallowed hard. "Ten years ago you gave up your dream. Don't you think your turn has come?"

Pursing her lips, she looked again toward the brightly lit barn. "It's too late for me. But it's not too late for Chance."

A lump formed in the pit of his stomach. "Please, Sera. Think about what you're doing."

"All I ever do is think, Alex. The time has come to stop thinking about what might have been. That's all in the past. I have to think of the future, and my future is here."

CHAPTER TWENTY-THREE

"RAINY MONDAYS." Sitting at the kitchen table, Max stared down into his coffee cup. "I should've trusted you to do the right thing. Just goes to prove, you're never too old to learn."

Alex switched on the light above the kitchen table before carrying over his coffee and a box of baked goods. Though the sun had been up a half hour, the heavy cloud cover held the house in darkness. "I wasn't coming home much in those days. You couldn't know."

"When your children are small, you can keep a close eye on them. But once you're off to college—" Max shook his head "—you're influenced by others' opinions. I didn't know what to think, especially after you turned down my job offer in favor of Oliver and Associates."

Sitting across from his father, he opened the pink bakery box and withdrew a bear claw. "Mom's taking it easy on you with the goodies." He held the box open until his father got his own pastry.

"She's glad we're talking."

"Me, too." Alex glanced across the table and caught his father's brief nod. They sat in the quiet kitchen enjoying their breakfast.

"You know, I'm not one of those guys who just dwells on retirement." Dabbing his mouth with a paper napkin, Max leaned back in his chair. He combed a hand through his thick white hair.

"I know. What makes you say that?" Alex glanced at the clock, glad he still had plenty of time with his parents before heading back to the city. They had spent Sunday together.

"Your friend Carrie mentioned something yesterday about her taking some time off."

"You could've knocked me over with a feather." As soon as the words were out of his mouth he realized he had picked up the saying from Sera and her brother. His heart skipped a beat at the thought he might never see her again. "I had no idea she and Will were together, much less getting married and starting a family."

"You had other things on your mind."

Alex grinned, but let the grin fade away as he remembered his failed attempt with Sera. "Carrie asked if I minded taking over her cases sometime next year. I'm going to be in New York, so what does it matter?"

"How long do you plan to stay in the city?"

Busy inspecting the contents of the bakery box, Alex took a minute to process his father's question. He lowered the lid so he could see Max's face. "What do you mean? Until I come home for my next visit?"

Max shook his head. "Someday. When Carrie goes back to work. When I decide to cut back. I mean, this is the girl's home. Don't you want to come back someday?"

"If by *girl* you mean Sera, coming back in ten years won't make a difference. She'll still be running herself into the ground, still won't want to marry, unless she decides to marry some local guy."

"Like Cyrus?" Max motioned with one finger for Alex to open the box, then reached in and withdrew a peanut butter cookie.

"She doesn't love Cyrus. Besides, I think Cyrus has his sights set on the new vet. He's given up on buying Sera's farm—" Alex raised one eyebrow and shot his father a hard look "—at least, ever since your bombshell with Shawn."

Max tilted his head. "So if she doesn't love your cousin..."

Alex threw a whole cookie in his mouth. He allowed his father's comment to hang in the still air.

"As I was saying, maybe in five or ten years I might be thinking about cutting back." Max raised his eyes from the cookie on his plate to his son. "Do you think you might be thinking of making a change by then?"

Alex met his father's gaze across the kitchen table, over the pink bakery box, and thought about his father's unfinished sentence. He nodded. "Yes. That might work out, Dad. Thanks."

"RAINY MONDAYS. Good day to sit in the house and drink coffee." Shawn sat at the kitchen table and smiled at his mother. A fire glowed in the old cookstove, the heat steaming up the windows.

Sitting in the rocking chair, cup cradled in her hands, Hope returned his smile. "Without a doubt, son."

Sera couldn't believe how in all the years she had lived on the farm, she had failed to see the resemblance between mother and son. Now the similarities could be seen as plain as day. Both were small and wiry, both had the Callahan turquoise eyes and their wide smiles were exactly the same. How had she ever thought to take their home away from them?

"Listen to that boy." Hope leaned her head back and closed her eyes. "He sings like an angel."

Sera looked toward the empty hallway, the sound of her brother singing a lullaby drifting in from the den where he sat with his daughter. Now that Shawn's parentage was known, Sera understood Hope's strong feelings about bringing Bella home. She was happy for them all. For Shawn and Hope, for Chance and Bella. But as she glimpsed into the dark recesses of her coffee cup, she felt the familiar ache in her chest. Everything had changed for her family. Nothing had changed for her. She closed her eyes and breathed in the scent of rich coffee. Enjoy the simple things. She could do that.

"Are you still here?"

Sera looked up at her brother's voice. He stood in the doorway, his head almost touching the top of the frame. He and

Bella shared the same questioning expression, both staring at Sera.

She laughed at the sight, thinking, a woman, albeit a little woman, had finally tamed her brother. "Shawn said it's a good day to drink coffee." She raised her cup. *"Sláinte."*

Chance took Hope's cup and set it on the counter and then settled his daughter in his great-aunt's lap. He got a cup for himself and brought it over to the table, where he straddled a chair next to Sera. "It's a good day to fly."

"Are you kidding?" Sera glanced out the window and back at her brother. "It's a terrible day to…" At his warm, knowing smile she caught his drift. "Alex is flying out today."

"In Friday, out Monday." Snatching Sera's half-eaten toast off her plate, Chance finished Sera's breakfast in one bite.

Familiar irritation jagged her as she watched her breakfast disappear. "Do you mind?"

Chance continued as if she hadn't spoken. "The flight's not usually full. Not many people from the area go to New York City on a Monday. You could probably buy a ticket last minute." He glanced at his watch. "If you leave now, that is. Old Blue is fast, but you should be careful with the wet roads."

Sera took a breath and tried to interpret her brother's sudden interest in flight schedules. "Are you leaving? Is that what you're telling me?"

"For a smart girl, sometimes you can be so slow, sis." He glanced at Hope and Shawn and rolled his eyes. "I'm not going anywhere. You'd be a fool not to take that scholarship."

"How do you…?" Sera looked around the familiar kitchen. The dogs lay snoring on their beds. The fire burned in the cookstove. She looked at her brother, deciding the time to be honest had come. "I can't trust you to stay here, Chance."

Her brother nodded. "I never told you about some advice I got from one of the old-timers at the Opry." His gaze landed on his baby, who was talking gibberish, as if trying to contribute to the conversation. "He said I wasn't ready, that I needed to find my voice, find out who I am. So that's what I'm going to do. Sing local, maybe write some songs and raise my girl."

Sera looked up at the rooster clock over the sink. If she hurried... "No, it's a bad idea." She glanced at each of them in turn. "Isn't it?"

"I think it's a great idea." Hope's eyes twinkled. "Catch him just before he gets on the plane? I wish I could be there to see that."

"What are you waiting for, sis? For once in your life, take a chance. Gamble your heart." His face lit. "Hey, that's a good song title."

Leaving her brother muttering lyrics, she grabbed her yellow poncho from the hook and opened the door.

"Don't forget your shoes," her brother warned.

She grabbed the nearest footwear, her bright green rubber boots. Hopping on one foot, she jammed her feet into the boots. Chance grabbed her big purse, put it in her hands and kissed her cheek. "Good luck."

Running across the open space between the trellis and the barn, Sera's heart pounded in her chest. She was seriously short of breath when she jumped in the old truck. As if supporting her adventure, Old Blue started on the first try. She drove past the mock orange bush, past the big silver maple and down the long drive. At the end of the drive she hung a left. She gripped the steering wheel tightly. One thought on her mind. Finding Alex. The time had come. Her time had come.

She pulled up to the departure gate and jumped out of the truck. Running through the doors, she threw her keys in a high arc over a trio of college students to Scooby. "Take my truck. I'm not coming back."

Smiling, Scooby scooped the keys out of the air. "Can I rent it out?"

Passing a woman carrying an overflowing bag of knitting, she ran up to the ticket counter. “I need a ticket to New York.”

The agent was new and looked at her with suspicion. “The next flight out is in four hours.”

Sera looked up at the board. “I want the flight that’s boarding now.”

“We don’t have time to process luggage—”

“No luggage.” Sera dropped her driver’s license and credit card on the counter.

The woman hesitated. Her eyes darted sideways as if looking for help.

Sera leaned across the counter and lowered her voice. “There’s a man getting on this plane. He asked me to go with him and I said no, but now…” She looked sideways. The woman with the bag of knitting had one ear tilted in her direction. She looked back at the agent, whose eyes sparkled, whether with excitement or concern Sera couldn’t tell. “I’ve changed my mind.”

The agent suddenly straightened. "Well, why didn't you say you needed to be on the love plane?" The machine chattered out a ticket and she handed it, along with the credit card and driver's license, to Sera. "You better run, Miss Callahan."

Sera didn't waste a second and ran down the hall to security. She bypassed the line for the flight to Detroit.

"Hey, lady!" A husky man in the act of removing his shoes reached out for her.

"Sorry. Emergency." Sera tossed her boots on the belt, shoved her ticket into Al's hands and stepped into the scanner. The woman with the wand glared at her. "What's your hurry?"

"She's good, Gretta. Let her through." Al gave her a smile. "The lady's on a mission."

Gretta nodded grudgingly. "Go ahead."

Sera hurried toward the glass doors.

"Sera, your ticket."

She plucked the ticket from Al's fingers and kept going. When she stepped on a stone outside, she winced and realized she had forgotten her boots. But her objective was in sight. Alex stood at the base of the stairs leading to the plane, one foot on the first step and one hand on the railing.

"Alex, wait." Sera stopped. The men loading the baggage cart gave her a glance and then looked at each other nervously.

Alex took another step.

Releasing a deep breath, Sera shouted, "Alex, wait!"

Her breath seized in her chest as did everything else. Like a freeze-frame, everyone except Sera and Alex seemed locked in place. He turned so slowly she was sure she would faint from a lack of air by the time their eyes met.

But she was still standing.

Alex released his hold on the railing and took one step toward her.

Sera smiled. Tears sprang to her eyes, appreciating that this short distance between them was the distance from one life to another.

Alex dropped his bag to the tarmac and ran to her.

Sera held out her arms, and he caught her and swung her around before setting her back down.

He looked deep into her eyes. "Sera, you're barefoot."

Al came rushing out, holding the bright green boots in the air. "I've got them, Alex."

He handed them to Alex and then backed away. He waved off the baggage handler bent on disrupting the two.

"I thought of something we have in common." Sera tightened her arms around Alex's neck. She had no intention of letting go.

Alex held her close and smiled at her. "Thank goodness. I was afraid we were hopeless. What do we have in common, my love?"

At his term of endearment, Sera almost lost her ability to speak. "I love you, too, Alex."

Alex bent down and touched her lips

with his. The cold rain, the warm lips. All familiar. “You’re coming with me, then? You’re flying to New York? On a plane? In the rain?”

“All of the above.” She beamed. “I’m not afraid to take a risk anymore, Alex. I guess gambling is in my genes after all.”

“Some things are a safe bet.” He carried her over to the stairs and gently placed her on the steps. Then, kneeling, he slipped a rubber boot onto her bare foot. “You know, while I’m down here…”

She *was* Cinderella. “Yes, Alex. A thousand times, yes.”

* * * * *

If you enjoyed this touching romance from author T. R. McClure, don’t miss her other terrific Harlequin Heartwarming titles:

AN ALLEGHENY HOMECOMING
WANTED: THE PERFECT MOM

Available from www.Harlequin.com